T0022283

A Sun to Be Sewn

A Sun to Be Sewn

JEAN D'AMÉRIQUE

Translated from the French
by Thierry Kehou

Other Press

NEW YORK

Originally published in French as *Soleil à coudre*
in 2021 by Actes Sud, Paris
Copyright © Actes Sud, 2021

English translation copyright © Thierry Kehou, 2023

Epigraph from "So Many Tears" by 2Pac, from *Me Against the World*, 1995.
Poetry excerpt on page 20 from "Michaëlle" by Kettly Mars, in *Anthologie de poésie haïtienne contemporaine: 73 poètes*, James Noël, ed. Paris: Points, 2015.

Production editor: Yvonne E. Cárdenas
Text designer: Jennifer Daddio / Bookmark Design & Media Inc.
This book was set in Cochin and Rough Love
by Alpha Design & Composition of Pittsfield, NH

1 3 5 7 9 10 8 6 4 2

Library of Congress Cataloging-in-Publication Data
Names: Amérique, Jean d', 1994- author. | Kehou, Thierry, translator.
Title: A sun to be sewn : a novel / Jean D'Amérique ; translated from the French by Thierry Kehou.
Other titles: Soleil à coudre. English
Description: New York : Other Press, 2023. | Originally published in French as Soleil à coudre in 2021 by Actes Sud, Paris.
Identifiers: LCCN 2022034921 (print) | LCCN 2022034922 (ebook) | ISBN 9781635422825 (paperback) | ISBN 9781635422832 (ebook)
Subjects: LCGFT: Novels.
Classification: LCC PQ3949.3.A46 S6513 2023 (print) | LCC PQ3949.3.A46 (ebook) | DDC 843/.92—dc23/eng/20221130
LC record available at https://lccn.loc.gov/2022034921
LC ebook record available at https://lccn.loc.gov/2022034922

FOR

Makenzy Orcel

FRÈRE-VOLCAN

Will I survive 'til the morning
to see the sun?

—TUPAC SHAKUR

They're crazy, these birds criss-crossing my mind. Their wings, an archipelago of fire. Their singing, a rolling hill of turbulent skies. Messengers of light, without a doubt, who cause the memory of the touch against my skin on the last day of class to beat even louder inside of me. But, as usual, I still can't capture some small glimmer of this godsend, I still can't put to paper this flash of lightning that expands into a chill in my arteries. Words crossed out. I'm making a kingdom of crumpled papers.

Papa puts on his robe of anger to get us worked up, to mess with our heads. A brief reminder of the purpose of his mouth, a machine gun on the lookout for the slightest opportunity. Blood open to fire, he rants and raves, drifts in his own storm, gives his whole body over to a violent tirade, and yells like he has never been yelled at, even in his childhood. If childhood is the age of silence, as he believes, then he didn't have an actual childhood. The most elusive chapter of his story that comes to mind is his alliance with the streets. And as the Angel of

Metal says, you're not a child anymore when the streets are the only one cradling you.

Papa stretches out under the roof, a raging wave. Outside, the sky gathers into a web of lace. The day's dying light hangs its veil silently on the end of an invisible wind. It's the night that has come to let us know. Streaming shadows soak up the sunset. The well-known uproar from our mouths that marks the restoring of electricity hasn't kicked off yet. Usually, if we've already put something in our stomachs and still have five gourdes left, we buy ourselves a candle to erode the darkness. It's our way of atoning for the days marked with basic light. Electricity, we don't expect it every day. There's hardly any of it, a common absence around here, like fathers in the household. The azure is fading, not a star to keep our eyes under the illusion of the blue sky, it contaminates the heart of the house. It's the flashlight of a phone that helps us shine a hole onto the skin of the shadowy visitor.

You'll be…

If his cell phone's dead, he'll be more than just a little upset. There's no way he's missing a single call. Papa lands an impressive slap to my head and snatches his phone, which I was using to

light up the room. He definitely would've ripped
my arm off with it if he could. I try not to cry,
fearing the onslaught isn't over. Instead, I scurry
to scoop up off the floor the papers on which I
was accusing language for its painful failure,
right before Hurricane Papa put an end to it.
Will I ever finish this letter? Orange Blossom,
my mother, retreats to the far side of the room.
She doesn't dare to speak, has never dared to cut
out her lifeless tongue. Years of silence that she's
blind to, an eternity she's suffered her whole life.
My mother holds her words, to avoid plunging
her mouth back into bitter beginnings. Silence,
then violence. No: violence, then silence. Orange
Blossom is afraid to break the ice, she pretends
she doesn't see anything, she defies her emotional
charge by wringing out the laundry, which now
sings louder at the ends of her gripped hands.
She's lucky to be a bit far away, otherwise she'd
crumble under the executioner's muscles. The
executioner who her mouth can't name.

You'll be... You'll be alone.

Casket of tenderness, Papa feels life coursing
through his body only when he hits. To hit...
Protecting against the blows is pointless. The
poetics of the fist. I strike, therefore I am. Papa

doesn't care for soft games. He dislikes all things that don't, according to him, hurt the muscles enough. He can't stand literature, for example. For him, to write would be a real insult to his body. He isn't one of those people who opens their window to poetry. *Poets have enormous fists*: he'd make Lavilliers think twice about ever singing this verse. He doesn't have a feel for words. One day, as he sat watching a writer ramble on TV—it's not that he didn't understand the writer's comments, it's just that the man disgusted him for being content with being a writer—he growled at the screen like a sphinx: Maybe if you thought about other things besides expanding your bibliography, if you threw as many punches as you did words, maybe you'd take down a good chunk of these assholes you'd like to see shut up!

The heart of the neighborhood beats to the rhythm of nothingness. Shadows branch out relentlessly, until forming one of those nights where the last glow of the retinas perishes. One of those heavy nights that you feel pulling on the clock to abort dawn's dreams. One of those nights that gives the street its formidable attire.

Night lets her silence flow at the mercy of the concrete while the guns conduct the symphony.

I look again at the page, I insist, I invite the song to couple with my voice: How to spell beyond the alphabets of emptiness, this feeling that boils in my blood? Papa, lying on a small bench in front of the door, resumes one of his routine gestures: from his lips, he lifts a red dot that erodes only a small patch of the darkness that contorts the space. Horseman of the clouds, he raises his joint to the sky, as if he were trying to draw the attention of the god that the legend of the mouth that gives and the ear that receives has been hiding there for ages. Papa ignores him, but it seems like the Most High captures him in his sight line, hoping he'll bless him with a puff. Who knows, maybe he weeps for a little bit of cannabis. Go figure where the phenomenon of rain comes from ... Poor God! They accused him of having created everything, yet he's fascinated by a simple plant that can make him journey beyond the stars, beyond the sad sky where humans have relegated him to.

You'll be ... You'll be alone.

My mother tries to raise her gaze, shackled under the scrap metal of fear. A frail glance behind Papa's back, then head down—you can feel her harvesting a deep wound, her eyes producing streams of water complicit in a heavy silence.

While his clothes occupy Orange Blossom's hands in a basin, Papa tries to concentrate on the smoke that he steers with an acrobatic breath. But difficult to achieve. Forever haunted by an important question, trapped between his own enclaves, eternal cobwebs where his soul remains coiled. A question that comes back to him each time he has the misfortune to reflect on the life that he harbors. What have I done with my human light? That is his wound. He'd like to dig into his soul, plunge into his inner mirror, imagine himself otherwise, jump on his scattered fragments. But it's a waste of time to lure this reflection which he never knew how to catch. That's to shatter against the smirk of life. He curses his thoughts. The obsession with guns already impregnates him more than his reason. He no longer even polishes the metal. Papa sees beautiful promises shining in the drops of blood that cover it. A return to the red thread of his life.

The door to the room would surely want to punish him for slamming it so hard on his way out. The noise that emanates extends in the same virulence as the voice of Papa hurling one last address at me. *You'll be…*

ou'll be alone in the great night. It's not the first time I've heard this phrase. It makes my veins itch. I've always tried, and still try, to understand its meaning. Papa repeats it to me often, it flows in his fury against me like the thread of a destiny stretched to my throat.

I finish my piece of bread and my glass of sweetened water, then lie down on what we dare call a bed, I mean, something that barely separates the body from the floor. You have to rub shoulders with poverty to know this. Or just have lived in this city on the night of the twelfth day of the year that began the second decade of the twenty-first century. The bodies that caressed the concrete. The skin surrendered to the pleasure of the pavement. Without any reluctance. After the frenetic revolt of the walls, conquering the night on the bare floor was becoming the inevitable outlook of an entire people.

Mom seems to be done with the laundry. But I still don't feel her warmth next to me. I'll still have to wait to enjoy this moment where I feel safe when she lies down next to me. I hear her pouring rum. She likes to drink to allow her insomnia flowers to grow.

In my head, I rebuild the circle of my life, imagine all the holes where I could crash to sleep, get away from the world for a few hours. It's not enough. The day lingers in my retina, my eyelids still stand on the battlefield. Before me a tough climb to orchestrate. Papa and his tune are slashing my soul. *You'll be . . .* I shatter against the dense evening, I don't know how to finish my letter, I don't know how to lay my heart on the page. For a long time, bitter shadows have stolen my words, a river of silence flows through me. How do I address my mirror-heart, how can I declare my love for this being who's burning my veins? I exhaust myself, while the clock ticks too slowly. I spend time tossing and turning my body, before finally falling on sleep's doorstep.

The night waters my nightmares all the way through the morning.

The sun gently greets the walls, splits the door, and nestles its glow inside the room. I unfold my eyelids. I won't have seen my mother in that first glow of the day. I change out of my raggedy clothes with their taste of the night, restore my face with the magic of a large cup of water, and still tend to my teeth with a tired brush and without the use of toothpaste. It's been a ritual for a long time. I wash. Because I'm dressed in the traces of a dirty life. Because my sky loiters beneath muddy clouds. I wash. I learned to wash, to wash despite everything.

*E*ver since I was little, my mother never misses an opportunity to instill in me principles, which she considers more necessary than anything else in life. You don't stay dirty, Cracked Head! Pain already eats at you inside, you don't need to advertise it. Your guts, your blood, they bathe in shadow. At least keep the sun on your lips, let the light shine on your skin. Wash yourself, my girl. There. To wash myself despite everything… I kept her words, or rather her words kept me, I don't know. Anyway, childhood is a wound that can't be washed away.

I could've washed myself much better if water was counted on as a right for me. A fountain five hundred meters away, and when I arrive with my bucket, I still have to contend with fifty other people. The fight, similar to the waltz of nocturnal dogs in the urban areas. Not the struggle, the fight. If we were talking about a struggle, we could take it in the veins. We could amass all our torn energies to turn things around. Vomit our thirst against city hall. The struggle for water. To finally have a drink of our rights. But every day we endorse a struggle that breaks against our own faces. We take up causes that don't go beyond the walls of the district, that don't even go beyond the flanks of this fountain.

To exert myself for four hours like I did yesterday—between verbal outrage and savage confrontation of the body—to bring back one bucket of water. I can't set out on this path before I leave for school this morning.

've never depended on this life to live. It's not an illusory circle like school that's going to

rip me away from this walk. School is without a
doubt the most rotten nonsense that our worlds,
however, seek to illuminate. At least that's what
the schools in my country tell me. Endless rules,
like thorns under our tender footsteps. Nothing
to do with the fucking life that awaits us just at
the end of the street. With its charter renewed
with every fading moment. We learn to count
at school, elsewhere others fabricate statistics.
Some sign big contracts they can't even read,
others would give their lives to learn to decipher
letters, to learn to read in one of these schools in
the area: Holy Ruin Mother of Bourdin School,
Crop Top Middle School, Sisters of Stain and
Slut, Bogus Academy, Eew Middle School, or
even the St. Facial Seminary, which I attend.

To teach me? I'm well educated on the
damages of my world, on its decadent allure
and its obscene antics that stalk the last line of
human defense. I come here for two reasons: to
answer the lie of a society selling diplomas and
especially to look out for the moon of my life, she
who regulates my chills.

The teacher digs deep into his reserve of
saliva and insists that we take him seriously,

as if the happy geometry of life emanated from his mouth. We know what pattern to draw, we solve all the problems here, we invent a world of deceptions and we start to believe it. And so we put barricades on our own trails, a harsh gray in front of our dreams of whiteness. Thousands of mirages at the mouths of our eyes. Everything we learn here has nothing to do with what's happening elsewhere, outside of this building. As if we were going to stay stuck in the world of school. As if we were just derelicts, not giving a shit about a spirit that'd keep us standing in the face of life.

*N*o matter how hard you try to put your so-called knowledge in the service of the community, you ignore extremely important things, things about yourself. You'd do better spewing on us as quickly as possible those notes of your so-called history lessons, which clearly haunt your brain, instead of force-feeding us your morals. You'd do better ripping out that perverse eye that you direct at me every day. You'd do better not inviting me into your car, not promising me anything again. You'd do better putting away your fake smiles, your little hand games in the wake of my body. Monsieur, do you know I work for those who snatched your daughter's computer and trendy cell phone last week? Do you know that my tuition fees are paid for thanks to this type of activity? What do you think? You think I've got a father, a mother who slaves to pay bundles in exchange for your rotten brand of education?

I could've spoken in these terms, I could've told the teacher everything. But I'm afraid, too afraid to enter into the night. *You'll be...*

Papa is the one who led the execution of the plan. He asked me the night before to identify the students who had the latest expensive electronic gadgets. And, as usual, I applied myself. I put Silence on my list. To successfully carry out the operations, I play an antenna role: I've got to provide Papa with all the information he needs to apprehend the targets or find very subtle ways to lead them straight to him somewhere. Last week I had to deal with the case of Silence. A huge anguish for me—I'm so crazy about this girl. If only Papa knew... But even if he knew, he wouldn't care. *You'll be alone.* Papa doesn't fool around. Tin under the flesh, concrete in the palm, heavy stones in his speech, he's a man who got off to a bad start in the human bubble. When he walks by, tenderness prefers to step aside. Even the rain, when it no longer has any strength, ends up falling. Papa doesn't abdicate his inferno of anger, nor does he stop climbing the floors of violence. If red is trumps, then his star sleeps in blood. He breaks the strings when the guitar begs for swing. So I follow Papa's orders, albeit reluctantly. He himself is just fulfilling the wishes of his boss, the Angel of Metal. The latter is the most influential boss that we have ever known, his legend burns all the tongues of our neighborhood, and his reputation goes even beyond that. No need to tell you you have to bow to his authority. At any rate, Papa, like his other soldiers, doesn't negotiate his commandments.

On the day of the holdup, Papa stayed on the lookout in the street, in front of the school, waiting for the assist from me to finish the play. And I didn't have any room for error, I had to bring him Silence, one way or another. It wasn't an easy thing, since she's always under her father's arm.

Here I am in the heat of the moment. When the teacher goes to get his car in the parking lot, I take advantage and approach Silence, who waits for him in the courtyard near the school's

exit. I know that her father doesn't allow her to
have relationships with other students, especially
if they're from the sorry slums like me, Cracked
Head, from the City of God. I walk towards her,
my face distraught by shyness. A slight smile
sprung from her lips, an invitation to a journey
towards the light. I ask her if she doesn't mind
taking a picture of me. Without hesitation, she
acquiesces with a gesture of the head. In her
eyes, I get a glimpse of a rare blue sky. Her gaze
cuts through me. Without saying a word, she
takes my hand: it's tenderness visiting me. A
fever seizes my body. I feel my heart beating, dry
wood cracking. I'd go much further with Silence
in this surge of desire that I feel consuming us
alive, but I'm on a mission… We go through the
gate, and here we are outside. While Silence
pulls out her phone to take a picture of me, Papa
approaches and puts the cold steel against her
temple and snatches the phone from her as well
as the backpack containing her computer. A few
seconds is all it took. He then gets back on his
motorcycle and tears up the dirt road, a white
cloud of dust trailing him into the distance. Tears
flood Silence's cheeks. I welcome her into my
arms, to calm her tremors. I try to pretend to be
stunned at what just happened, but by squeezing
her in my arms, the emotion takes me away for

real. The teacher arrives. As he gets out of his car, those who saw the robbery inform him of the situation. He tears his daughter off my arms while glaring at me with contempt.

I've got roses lodged in my heart for Silence, butterflies in the corner of my eyes to draw for her, I dream of having the tenderness of flowers to get close to her beauty, I hope to turn into dew to accommodate her at dawn. I've been digging up my being for a long time in search of a verb that can express to her my love in due form, but what I feel refuses my language, my ink remains muzzled by silence. I'm hot-blooded for this girl, and ever since I've been around her on this earth, I'm nothing more than a body strewn with chills. She's my moon. I didn't want to add my fire to her wound, but my will is worth nothing. Like the Angel of Metal, when Papa gives you a job, he doesn't ask you to love him. *You'll be alone in the great night.* I suspected this sentence would come back to hammer my mind. All I did was obey. Maybe after I wanted to die. Of course I could die. I could offer myself eternal silence, like my father with his Beretta on the day I was born—according to what the legend of the mouth that gives and the ear that receives has to say. I'm young, I know, I've got suns to raise on the sides of my road. But, deprived of my human share, I might not have a coffin for my thirst to die in.

'm on my way home after a long day of school. The sun hits like an ax in my skull. I need some good ice cream to mitigate this heat, but the street vendor from the corner doesn't show up today. I cross my neighborhood, the smell of rotting flesh and a procession of flies enveloping me, and I ask myself for the umpteenth time this question: Will an education be able to pull me away from this filthy slum one day?

Coming from all parts of the country, their ass whupped by social wounds, a human tide arrived here in the name of light on a day of black skies, a day of pale faces. Nomadic like a wave, free, if freedom is taking back what the power-hungry wrongfully privatize. A crowd of rejects arrived in this corner on a day of torn sun. A day of struggle, to mark the windows of History with one hell of a milestone. A day of raised fists, to plant a flag of flames on the hills of memory. The marginalized arrived in hordes and settled, offering themselves a plot of land to assert their right as inhabitants of the earth. A day to resent cowardice, a day to spit on the

State that had declared itself the owner, leaving vacant lands at the mercy of creatures and waste while thousands of citizens were homeless. About two decades ago, a human tide arrived here to force the city out to sea, to push the ocean and create a residential row, uninhabitable, however.

Neighborhood, if this is one, at the punctured heart of a garbage dump, an avalanche of shit where some remember a river. Less than ten meters from Pool of Water Theater, the only theater—which isn't really one unless theater is a hell—that the State has set up, this pool of filth offering a singular spectacle at the slightest rain, seems to have landed in the right place. Still, it's our calling card. When we arrive on Bicentenaire Boulevard, we see, with no effort, an army of debris going off towards the sea in a slow march, an army whose primary weapon is a nose-smashing smell. We can follow it, we can follow it to get all the way home. We're used to leaving with it, to going to some unspeakable place, to going every day towards a place where we lose ourselves. We walk along the terrible Bois-de-Chêne ravine, pilgrims of decadence. We're from a city that walks in its strayed steps, we're from a country that sails towards its ruins. It's by walking that we come across our own patterns, *it's by walking that our life goes away with the pebbles of Bois-de-Chêne*, like in Kettly Mars's poem.

A space braided in the light of all kinds of misfortunes, not even spared from God. Here, it's the City of God. Dirty neighborhood, in the image of its last name.

As I walk through the door, a cigarette butt falls short of my face. What a way to greet someone. A thousand trips in my head leaf through the history of our relationship, but nothing indicates why she'd do that to me; she says sorry, grabbing my head with an almost tender hand. I shudder at this unusual gesture.

Yes, I'm okay, Mom...

On the table, a half bottle of five-star rum. Her face says she'll be done with it before the agony of sun.

Orange Blossom made her first dives into alcohol at fourteen years old. One beer, just one beer, no more. Time was drinking its way, and these words hadn't had time for a refrain. A glass of *clairin* could follow. Sips don't last forever, so she multiplied them. Then she was mopping up several bottles of wine in a day, traversing the night in a stream of whiskey. All that was made of glass ended up winning the heart of her hand. There was no more inventory. Twenty-four years later, today, she no longer knows how to measure these waves that she sends to rule in her blood. As if time were only good for drilling holes in the bottom of her. Her soul takes refuge at the slightest concern. Drowning, she said, is the best path to draw your halo from the abyss. She launches into her tipsy flow to seize her light, drinks against the time and the life that frame her pain. Her body turned into a party for the booze. My mother, this canoe navigating on drunkenness itself... If I had been the first seed to grow inside her belly, the world of the living would've missed me. After getting pregnant the first time, she had an abortion because, according to Hippocrates' dirty doctors, she couldn't keep the child and continue to drink.

*N*ight.
What's this shit doing on the table, Cracked Head? How many times have I told you not to pile your papers here? We don't need to know if you're studying, if you're doing your homework or not, plus this table isn't made for that.

When Papa speaks, I have a hard time replying. I grab the white papers and the pen, and retreat to a corner, on the little rug, to try to sew a horizon in the image of my vow for Silence. What does my heart say? I get down to stirring it but my tongue doesn't know how to frame its flow. If only I could find the words to burn this void . . .

And my mother over there can't know my pain, she honors the bottle.

No mystery there. Those two red puddles in the eye sockets will tell you what color her night was. A night with the Politician whose ass is made for every chair, a man ready to trade everything to stay in power. Except the flesh of this woman, whom he met one rainy evening in a street saturated with rubbish from the capital.

More faithful to her positions than his own, he renounced his ideologies for a seat in government but didn't let go of Orange Blossom. Even after a botched blow job. Even after a blow job that made him holler just as he was picking up his phone. Last night my mother was at his house replaying what she's been doing for five years: surrendering her body to all of mister's obscene fantasies.

Luckily Papa wasn't there when my mom came home. He'd have waited for her at the door to bless her with an incredible beating. When, without warning, my mother spends the night out to work, her executioner, for lack of sexual prey, is capable of jerking off out loud in the middle of the house, spraying the floor and walls with cum, and waiting, leather belt in hand and veins on fire, for Orange Blossom.

The Politician whose ass is made for every chair never gets tired of fucking her. His whole body has been dripping with desire since his first encounter with Orange Blossom. That day, he'd lowered the windows of his official car to better appreciate her breasts before soliciting her. Immediately he was seduced by the well-planted islands in her corsage, these cathedrals perched on the chest, proud of the power of pleasure that made them swell, proud to be the source that provoked thirst in all those faithful to pleasure. Anyway, he hadn't looked much further, he wasn't interested in meeting the person behind the body. The Politician whose ass is made for every chair then became one of three clients for Orange Blossom, who was set from there on out. There was fire in the eyes of her sun.

Since the day she threw herself out onto the sidewalks of Grand-Rue like a lamppost that no longer lights up, Orange Blossom had told herself she needed a fixed income for this back-and-forth work. A salary of flesh, worthy of the energy spent by her body. She'd made it a point to excel in her customer service, to devote herself with skill to the care of the libido in order to obtain long-term arrangements, arrangements that were more durable than the trickle of certain men, as solid as the boner of those who resorted to strange formulations to delay their orgasm, believing with as much strength as their Glock-balls that sexual performance is linked to this capacity. Only she knows how many faces had promised to reappear in her sphere, how many bodies had promised to multiply their visits.

Those whom she never saw again. Until she fell on the Divine, then on the Lord of the Groin, her first two loyal clients.

The Divine practices fraud in public offices; she gets rich off the stupidity of others. Easy to imagine her fortune. Stingy like no other, she only gives Orange Blossom two thousand five hundred gourdes per month. The Lord of the Groin, he only pays three thousand five hundred gourdes. He claims that, in fact, he's the one who should be paid since the whole town recognizes him for his special talent of working the crotch ... Months passed before Orange Blossom met her third client and finally abandoned the slog of the sidewalk, an abusive adventure that many *filles de joie*—or rather of melancholy—experience even before adolescence. The Politician whose ass is made for every chair, the most generous, pays Orange Blossom five thousand gourdes per month. Sometimes with bonuses. Like those thousand gourdes last night, to mark yet another sensual escapade and for which she allowed him to kiss. Far from his wife, who for some time he can no longer honor with his sex. It's been five years since he exiled her with their daughter to Montreal, so as not to stain them with his political mud.

———

*O*range Blossom, leaving one world to dive into another. So goes the movement of her life, towards an opaque horizon banished far from the lighthouses. Last night, she was a hole, and let the Politician whose ass is made for every chair come inside her towards himself. Now, to try to find herself, and in her turn the prey of a large hole, she traces in herself an abyss and merges with the ocean. Her spleen needing a wash, she dries out the bottle with one last drink. It's downed in one swig.

It must also be said that her work led
her into many pitfalls. A pretty scathing
charge had been mounted against her, like
a wild flame concocted in the middle of a forest.
Eyes shrouded in repugnance and contempt
followed her. The whores of the open-air brothel
where she was trying to make a living didn't
fail to lambaste her because she disturbed their
ethics and customs with her attitude. And when
she abandoned that market, they saw the fruits
of their rants as much as the confirmation of
an impostor in this strange passerby with the
insolent style. Orange Blossom always ran her
show far from the stage, distancing herself
from the street to camouflage her activities,
as if she had something to preserve, a spark
she refrained from displaying on her face. She
diverted her momentum as far away as she could
from the crowd of colleagues, and picked out
the lonely edges of the street to fish for clients.
The other hookers couldn't believe her disdain
for traditional ways, her walking the Grand-Rue
without embracing its history and its vices. They
remembered that when they arrived here they

were no more than the insignificant shadow of the stars they now embodied, they had to arm their wings with the experience of others to face the winds of the profession and take off, they had seen themselves obliged to mix their carnal potential with the teachings of the veterans to become street hookers.

This mood of divergence had sparked a cold war, the acrid scents of which had come to stifle the atmosphere of the brothel. Even the owner couldn't raise his voice to calm the discordant racket. What the hell is going on here? Come on, a little peace isn't gonna kill you! These words stayed lodged in his throat. But he didn't want to risk going bankrupt by disturbing these women in their wildness, so he shut up. The main thing for him, anyway, was to keep as many workers as possible to harvest the dollars; his interest was limited to the commission that he received on his filthy little rooms, where the girls completed the transactions with the customers they brought back from the street. The wound had thus gained in length. Orange Blossom no longer stood a chance to experience a break from the vitriol: her colleagues kept castigating her.

---

*O*ne day, Jenny Suintaxe, a prostitute recognized by her peers and customers for her passion as an exhibitionist, decided to coach Orange Blossom in a spectacular game, as much to provoke her as to show her the limits of her posture of infertile loneliness.

Here we are on a Tuesday, a dull afternoon, as pale as the faces of passersby colliding against grief after another empty day in the bowels of the city. The workers of the body, left with no other strategy, have tightened their nets. But the customers are still scarce. The young girl, or the one pretending to be one, appears on the scene that she's cooked up, gets rid of her clothes, allowing the strobe lights to watch over her crepuscular skin. She feels perfect amid the torn sound of the speakers that howl in the name of a variety of world voices—Beyoncé, Aya Nakamura, Yemi Alade, et cetera—to accompany the movement of the bodies. Under her sheet of nudity, the deliverer of pleasure draws a horizon riddled with sensual petals, capable of overwhelming the crotch of any person who'd come to lose themselves. She presses her hands against a wall at the entrance to the brothel, her back horizontal, and spreads her legs to let her ass float and half open a hole at the cut of her vagina.

A green snake crawls up her left thigh, its head follows one buttock and approaches Jenny's anus. It doesn't fail to shock visitors. She's been sporting this tattoo for three years, a striking reminder of her young career: she found herself, with ten other counterparts, on a boat off the coast of Jamaica delighting a female millionaire, who'd given her a bundle so that she'd accept this souvenir.

With intent displayed all over the fire of her body, Jenny increases her movements when she sees Orange Blossom arrive with a client. The young man, amazed by the flare of the show, refuses to continue towards the room where the carnal trafficking takes place, forgets and no longer listens to the woman who fished him off the side of the road, where he'd gone to rid his kidneys of that annoying water. He doesn't want to miss this show, would even like to join as an actor, and ends up complying when Jenny whispers to him: Give the money you were going to throw away and come take what you need, here and now. Overwhelmed by the all too troubling situation, Orange Blossom recomposes her face, stained with shame, makes her way towards the exit while tucking her bag under her arm, and goes home to think about how to face this stumbling block in the coming days.

*A*nother time, after a meeting, the general council of whores appealed to Charm de Pole, the man with the overflowing limb. The latter is known for abusing women uninformed of the calamity he drags between his legs. Everyone in the brothel got to know him. And afterwards, when he showed up, the hookers, dreading the massacre between their thighs, rewarded him with only a blow job. He was responsible for teaching Orange Blossom a lesson.

On the agreed evening, he arrived in the area and spotted in the crowd his target in front of the brothel. Excited by the mission, he doesn't need to be begged by the invitation of the sidewalk's tenant, all happy to drag this new client into one of those little rooms of fortune, where the worst awaits her nonetheless.

She complains about the enormity of her host's cock. After a thousand punishments, the condom still only contains half the load inside his chamber. Charm de Pole, the man with the overflowing limb, violently straddles Orange Blossom. The bed moans beneath the tumults. She screams, calls for help by exhausting a long list of people incapable of slowing down his tearing her: Jesus, Mother, Father, good Lord, my friends, my God, et cetera. She clears her throat, howls, howls so loud under the shipwreck which overwhelms her erogenous lands... Hearing her, they quickly realize that she's living a real martyrdom. The whores gathered in the area burst out laughing, rejoicing at the outcome of their plot. The crime is over, they are not moved by the atrocity. After thirty minutes, Charm de Pole comes back in a sweat. He's welcomed as a hero by his bosses, who promise him a free monthly blow job subscription as a reward.

A few minutes later, Orange Blossom comes out limping. The mocking eyes of her colleagues like needles pressed to her back. Her washed-out face evokes the aftermath of a violent earthquake...

All in all, Orange Blossom has lived through quite a few misfortunes during her sidewalk career. Among them, she even counts the worst possible one for a prostitute, according to her peers. When she was still a newbie in the profession, she very quickly fell in love with a man with whom she wasn't able to see herself as a commodity. Pregnant a few weeks later, she had to break from Grand-Rue for a while. Far from being a branch torn from its star, she has known mad love, but for nine months, no more. Nine months, and the spasms didn't delay in slicing her belly. Her lover took her to the hospital, and it was their last moment together. Once the child arrived, the doctors searched for the father for several long minutes to present it to him, but in vain. The guy had disappeared and never reappeared in my mother's life. In any case, Orange Blossom isn't capable of saying what became of him. When she talks to me, she doesn't stop saying *If your father were here…* and here's all I know: my dad isn't here. The legend of the mouth that gives and the ear that receives tells that this man detonated a Beretta on his temple on the very day of my birth, and that his body, a depositary of some mystical virtue, after stagnating for an hour in blood on the pavement, began to float in the air until he vanished behind the clouds… Me, I drift in the meanders of the city, I'm involved in the insides of the street, so I'm in the know about certain things that my mom doesn't know or doesn't tell me. Anyway, it's not from my mouth that she'll learn anything.

From my early childhood, I grew up in the arms of my mother's new companion, a man

that many take for my father. I call him Papa,
everyone calls him Papa, as if he were everyone's
father, but in truth he isn't my father, he's
nobody's father. I don't even know where this
nickname comes from, and I think no one has
dared ask him who doesn't wish to have children
why he lets others call him this. Anyway, it's
no surprise to people, around here, who aren't
familiar with the irony...

Dear Moon,

*The ink is poor, my hand dumb, and the paper
unsuitable. The impossible alone knows your
route, perhaps. I'm trying to braid the sky
between my fingers to write to you. The horizon
puts up a wall with each attempt. And now
this letter is two years old, the exact age of
the anguish that inhabits me in the face of the
difficulty to approach you. I write to you with
some delay in my throat. I speak to you with my
dead birds, my white veins, and my arched suns:
bitter fruits of the kilometers thrown between
our hearts. I try to move towards you, hoping
to see our desires melt into the same water. To
love you is the sweetest path through life. I move
forward. I've got burning inside me the memory
of our looks, of our joint heartbeats, still alive
in me that moment when we brushed against
each other last week, when you came out of class
holding your father's arm. And that day when
you took refuge on my chest . . . I can still hear
the bells of your heart ringing. I'm trembling.
I tremble, forgive me if my words come out
stumbling. Know that they were born with the*

mission of looking you straight into the eye and
telling you of my dreams to live there. I know
your gaze, it's the sea that watches over spring,
I can see the open sea every time I cross it and I
feel our impulses flare up, to bring down the high
walls that separate us. But your father acts as a
shield. I'm y

Another unsuccessful one, but I won't give up. One day my papers will stop ending up crumpled and I'll have this letter. One day, I'll know how to weave words in perfect form to address my moon. I mean it.

My mother tells me that at one time writing to give wings to a heart was elegance, that for a long time we wrote letters to each other, we declared our love on paper, and it was so beautiful, glowing.

For two years I've been staring at a piece of paper that I'd like to fill with tenderness.

I won't abandon the project. I'll write to my moon before nightfall. I'll write to her because I don't know what else to do. It's been a long time since I've been looking for a path towards my mirror-heart, the girl named Silence, but her father operates as a screen, he keeps her under his wing at school or locks her up in a luxurious house protected by an immense wall and a cohort of barbed wire. What to do? Write to her? I get started. All while asking: Even if I manage to transpose my fire into words, even if she receives my letter by some means, even if she responds with the same burst of light, will we really be able to meet? Will our bodies find the opportunity to burn, one with the other?

What to do?

My head is consumed.

I ask the wind to take away my torment, the ocean to drink my pain, and the instant to give me clarity. I call dawn to give me her hand.

Tomorrow is another night.

How many days like this will I go through? I surely would've done better to lock myself in a book, that might open me up to far more interesting horizons.

The end of classes, finally. The teacher calls me in to his administrator's office. Probably because this morning I insulted a classmate who'd made me angry. I'm already preparing myself to recopy the same sentence a thousand times, like the teacher asked me to do once when he deemed my behavior in his class to be disrespectful. He makes me wait. In the meantime, the school building has completely emptied out. Even Silence is already gone. Her mother came to pick her up by car.

Weird scenarios run through my head. Because according to the legend of the mouth that gives and the ear that receives, the teacher isn't very kind to little girls... And I think back to the perverse looks that he gave me sometimes, and I think back to that time when he invited me into his car, supposedly because he wanted to drop me off at my place, and I think back to the little hand game he once attempted on the horizon of my body… And I know, too, that he wasn't happy that day when he found Silence in my arms, after the holdup she'd suffered from Papa. I really want to get the hell out of here!

Suddenly, a vicious slamming of the door to the office rattles my mind: it's the start of a terrible nightmare. I hear a thunderous voice. If you scream, I'll kill you! I try to open my mouth anyway, but each attempt is shut down with a slap in the face. Then the teacher shows me his knife. I've got the impression he's going to slit my throat. I don't understand what's happening, but I keep silent, because I'm devoid of the slightest shield. He walks towards me and eventually overcomes my pathetic movements; despite my efforts to stop it, he manages to bind my arms and tie my legs to a chair. If I could, I'd kill myself at this exact moment, but even the windows of the afterlife are closed to me. The teacher forces me to watch him jerk off. How many knives take up residence in my soul? I feel torn on all sides. Now his penis intrudes into my mouth. The tragedy extends inside of me. I only have my teeth to tighten. An immense hole is being dug in my dignity. I'd have liked this to be a simple dream, so that at a given moment life can resurface intact from this horrible impasse.

Under the spigot in the courtyard, I wash my face to remove the teacher's slimy milk, the cigarette butt of his crime, before going through the exit. I leave dejected. A few hundred meters away from school, I start to vomit. Passersby offer me water to refresh me, make all kinds of hypotheses about my discomfort. I don't tell them the story, I'm busy sketching out what comes next...

For a long time the teacher has been preventing me from treading the space around Silence, and now he dares to attack me, contaminate my flesh and my intimacy. Can I continue to watch him do it? Certainly not. I spend the whole afternoon developing my battle plan. I'll neither go to the police station of shame, nor to the prosecutor's office of darkness, nor to the court of contempt, nor to our department of priced justice. My pride has already filed my complaint, this won't be a cold case. Tomorrow, my turn. Tomorrow, my justice. May the night bring me guidance and arms.

usk. The stage is set. Since yesterday, I've been waiting for this moment.

After an hour of roasting in the traffic jams on the big avenue, Monsieur swallows the last street. This street whose contours he's mastered because he's been taking it for over twenty years, ever since he's lived in this house, built thanks to a prestigious award from a foreign Catholic university. The Nissan pickup truck is brand-new and light on the asphalt, the seat comfortable. Monsieur, calm in his elsewhere, has no idea that a disaster awaits him at the end, the kind of danger for which you don't set up a red light. After rain comes good weather, but after good weather, it'll rain again. Monsieur doesn't know that the night has in store for him something other than the hug of a child who only knows how to obey and show love to her father, and the religious kiss of a woman tired of his absence. Just like he doesn't know that I don't give a shit about his school, which brainwashes minds in heaven's name, that I don't give a shit about his history classes, which spout morals instead of memory. He doesn't know that I'm behind this carcass of a car that borders the entrance of his house. Just like he doesn't know that under my waste-free gaze, which he crosses each day at school, there's a desire to blast his madman head, which believes it's civilizing students. Just like he doesn't know that he's preventing me from picking my flower on the other end of the shore, that I'd reach my other self, my mirror-heart, more easily if he wasn't always by her side. Just like he doesn't know I'm gonna bounce back after that assault he carried out against me, after that violent eruption in the flesh of my childhood, and that I intend to spit back at his face that bitter taste he stuck in my mouth against my will.

*M*onsieur isn't accompanied by a security guard. Contrary to what he thinks, it seems like his Lord isn't quite protecting him tonight. And so here my act takes shape. As I predicted, he gets out of his car to open the gate. In stride, I shatter the voices of reason and bring down the teacher. Two shots. One for the winter that houses his face, another for the nights that abound in his mind. Two shots that fire flawlessly. Two shots where my vengeance shines. One for his hold on his daughter, another for humiliating me, assaulting me. Two shots. A brutal song deployed into space to bloom high-pitched sounds. And life no longer knows how to resonate. The body chases its flamboyances. Lush splatters play their geometry against the glass. The pool takes off on the ground. I see the blue veils of my childhood tear in the red basin. It's the first time that my hand has executed such a disaster: to pierce flesh and to rattle breath. To break the needles of life. To pierce the flesh of the father of Silence, that girl who torments the left side of my chest. To disrupt the breath of the father of Silence, my moon, this star-girl that traverses the stream of my dreams with rosewater.

Once the act was completed, I hoped to throw the crime into the trails of oblivion. And yet, I quickly reclimb the hills of my childhood, where the banner of my failed homeland floats. Is this night here? *You'll be...*

know my cliffs, my shadowy neighborhoods. I'm not the least bit naked under the glow

of weapons. Papa taught me a lot about the
path of blood, about the waltz of the iron in the
territories of the hand. Dirty jobs, up until now,
I've accomplished a lot of them. Underneath the
school uniform, I make high-risk trafficking
possible. I deliver weapons on behalf of Papa.
From the street, I gather good leads on robberies
or kidnappings for him: the man who leaves class
before it's over, saying that he needs to go cash
a check; the pedantic boy who wants everyone
to know the price of his cell phone and other
electronic gadgets; the child who gets dropped
off at school in a luxury car and who doesn't
seem in any way to embody the fortune of the
parents. Narcotics infringe the gaze of cops
who mistake my lunch box for a delivery ship.
My books incubate the loads in my backpack.
Sometimes I don a mask, a 9 mm elongating
the arm, to supervise a hostage. A whole pile of
mud I've known how to wear on the forehead
throughout my life. But never had I pushed a
body towards eternal dust, never had I smashed
a breath, never had I killed anyone before the
teacher.

Now, a murder on my hands. Maybe it's the
last step that separated me from the climax of
a dark odyssey. The enamel on earthenware.
The absinthe of a star-studded career perfumes

me. I ruminate on my fractions of darkness,
torn between a glory stained with blood and the
simplicity of a blue sky that the flip side of this
life might offer me. Is this solitude? Is this night?
Is this what it's to be alone in the night? I can't
help but stir up the fact.

You'll be... You'll be alone.
You'll be alone in the great night.

Anyway, on the one hand I took revenge, on
the other I feel like I'm digging a path towards
my mirror, walking towards my moon...

I put the weapon away and the mask under
the books in my bag, and then disappear. I
prepare to get back on the avenue. I put on my
makeup of fear and join two adults running at
full speed, seemingly to escape the sob of the
bullets. They worry about me, wonder why
parents would let me out on the streets at this
hour when cannons are dethroning Morpheus.
I'm crying with them...

I'm on the bus but wandering on a block
of dark thoughts. My story, a catalog of
disasters, knocks on the back of my neck.
Returning to the corridors of my childhood, I
collect debris from splattered dreams. The bus

stops. The event is still young in my head. I get off.

This neighbor must be thinking of me by playing this gangsta rap record. I light a cigarette. Ass cheeks coddling a cinder block and back against the wall of the house, I stare at the emptiness. I roam beyond my inner drama for lack of eradicating it, dive into my own faraway, this slow hell I'm walking through, not without turbulence. When stars fall, the sky can't sew up their beauty. My stone cast already, how to shape the void? You have to believe that everything around me looks like night.

You'll be... It's coming back.

Me, Cracked Head, allegory of the thousand and one pains of the ghetto ... My quest for a vital symphony fails. Voice shipwrecked, now my breath echoes in a spiral of ills. Strange cacophony. My name is a poem about the end of the world.

Corrosive rays imprison the edges of my life, eat at me to the depths. Skin surrendered to the song of thorns, it's like I'm buried in an immense labyrinth and don't know where a breach will finally come to sketch a horizon for me. Like a candle imposing deadly tears onto itself, here I'm trafficked in the halos of violence, I strain my gaze until my eyes bleed. Lacerated to the very depths of the gut, I place an epitaph on the massacred flowers of my childhood. Frayed sails, broken wings in the storms of time.

Sometimes I understand people who, like my father and his beloved Beretta—according to the legend of the mouth that gives and the ear that receives—get up one day and blow their heads off once and for all.

My childhood, a herd of needles in the flesh of my lifetime. Miserable neighborhood, oh my City of God, I curse you for my dreams drawn up in lightning.

The violence flows, savage grammar. I've drunk some and it devoured my tongue. I loved my innocence, I still love it, I may fight against the beast that fills me. I promised my hands tenderness, but the iron got the best of me. Violence has conquered my white lines. A dirty history wounding my voice.

Is this how loneliness grabs me? Is this how night calls me? I hear the wild song, a chorus that is familiar to me. *You'll be... You'll be alone. You'll be alone in the great night.*

Pushing myself to climb over time with precocious steps, destroying myself with cruelty: I poison myself to be someone among these beasts who lie to themselves about their nature. To flee this world that's not looking good, escape these wounds that mark the interstices of the dream, to be at least a cry in the slaughterhouse: I won't perish in this bloody contract of mankind.

'm in pain. I'm in pain in my uniform. I'm more than just in pain in my skin.

Something is watching me. A furious noise deep down inside me. I apply myself with good measure, making myself as dark as possible. Not at all difficult, the dark being familiar to me. A sun to be sewn since my first cry in the world. Time gnaws, tangles the threads instead of weaving them. Life eternally in need of giving birth from its rainbow. Here I am, in this little church, among so many other souls who've come to *fulfill* a duty of sadness. Around me is the whole delegation of pupils from my school. I'm sitting, my eyes condemned to seek the essence of the ground since my arrival. No, I tell myself, eyes lowered, this isn't such a good way to hole up. And why should I want to hide here? I'm already in the vase, I just need to become one with the liquid.

As soon as I lift my head, I stumble on my hope of fresh water: Silence. Her eyes, like fireflies, illuminate the paleness between my eyelids. Spring dances in her pupils and the sun gives it a go, tightropes along her eyelashes. Her gaze, an expanse of sand here to sweet-talk the waves. What's left of summer, young lady, if your eyes bear so much warmth? I unleash a stainless smile to penetrate the windows of her heart. She opens a path for me. An improbable magic calls on us. Despite my desire for lightness, the gesture loses its thread of eternity. Because I'm hurting. I'm hurting in this crowd sitting under the roof of tears. A stampede of shrapnel under my skin. An urge to vomit that I can no longer hold back assaults me with tremendous pressure. Time to get out and run to the bathroom, I feel a tension consuming my flesh. You must always wash yourself, my mother often said, to tuck my childhood in despite its ugliness. I wash up. I wash my face after filling the toilet up by emptying my guts through my mouth.

I didn't think of closing the door behind me when I entered. She opens it and surprises me, then walks in and closes the door. All I've got left is the address of a chill. I find the soak of the gaze that bowled me over earlier. There's no detour, we're in the flesh. We're in the explosion of the dream. With an unprecedented gesture, she completes the silence that tears the room apart. Her fragile hands search for the quietude of my cheeks. The fire of her lips against mine, my whole body ignites. Here we are, Silence and I, interlaced. Upon contact with her anatomy, I feel the infinity of pleasure. Her body, a special delegate of tenderness. I take my finger, then my tongue, and begin to reinvent the geometry of her lower lips. She reciprocates the gesture with unparalleled gentleness. I penetrate the opening of her sex. A happy abyss that calls us. The path is warm. It weeps its thirst for our steps. A taste of eternity envelops us.

Burned are all my letters, burned are my unfinished sentences, erased is my long road of words, we're in the thick of the subject matter, our bodies are indulging in the best language possible.

The journey turns out to be long. I come back in a shortness of breath released at the right time. My moon drinks her cry beneath her dress, lifted and pulled back above her chest to clear a path.

We leave the bathroom to return to the confines of the church. We take up our respective places without exchanging a word. Silence rejoices in having cum with me, but she isn't allowed to display it on her face. To suit the duty of sadness imposed by the circumstances, she starts to cry. And I, too, cry for a better chorus with the crowd that'd come to pay their

final tribute to the teacher. To better get closer
to Silence. By voice. The voice can be a path to
the other. The voice or rather the sob that tries to
compensate for a look that I'm now searching for
only to come across its absence.

*T*he teacher's wife is quite courageous in her
remarks. Sobs, she doesn't have many to
extract from her throat, not too many screams
to draw from her gut. Tears do the job full-time.
A police investigation will be worth nothing, she
said, human justice is rotten, justice down here is
too rotten, the country's highest rank where the
teacher is going will know how to suspend and
restore the balance. And plus, there's no reason
to seek justice where one doesn't wish to return.

*S*he says it all, the teacher's wife, or almost
everything.
  Thursday will be sad, that she doesn't say,
doesn't know it, doesn't know how to say it.
Because she doesn't know that all Thursdays will
be sad for me. Soon it'll be Thursday. Thursday
will be sad. Sadder than a Sunday is for a girl

addressing a requiem to her father. My moon
will escape elsewhere. Silence will take the plane
on Thursday, will go to the United States with
her mother, will go plunge herself in the New
York water, never to leave it. Far from the land of
effortless lead. Far from the land of twelve-year-
old gangsters. Far from the island of endless,
dizzying chants. Far from the country where a
student murders her teacher. Let's take note, let's
be clear above all, that the teacher shoved his
penis into my twelve-year-old mouth...

All Thursdays will be sad for a girl who loses
sight of her beloved flesh, the one she only
touched on the day of the funeral of the man who
earned her her first murder. But you see, that's all I
retain from the words of the teacher's wife. Of her
words, only a legacy of torment remains. My lion's
share is the arsenic of my tomorrows. Bitterness
will eat at my table every Thursday.

You'll be... You'll be alone in the night. Am I face-
to-face with the real mirror? Is this what the night
looks like? Papa's disturbing record continues to
unfold in my head. A disaster phrase that'd long
held me hostage. And I've never managed to grasp
its meaning between the dark lines of my life.

he days are fading. My newly found lover is leaving. The footprints are still intense, I enjoy them and they make me cry at the same time. My days bear sadness for luggage. The bitter blood of this absence swirls in me, and the land of loneliness that inhabits me is so vast. I think about my lover for a day, my fleeting flame, my beloved of less than an hour, I think of the wonders that we're missing out on, I dream of Silence, I dream of my moon from my little neighborhood, from the City of God that is already a heavy burden to me. Who'll come to save me?

I live in Cité de Dieu, and it's neither a movie nor a fantasy novel. Here we see the thundershowers of destitution on the cheeks, the broken lines of looks, the chasm erected in the eyes, the mouths that express themselves in a vacuum, the so distant exile of bread, of education or of nutrition, the kids without sun on the horizon who crawl in the shadow of violence

and who'll become thugs to kill each other,
snatchers of breath, the relentless putrefaction
of the wound-season where one looks for a ray
of light, the eternal infernal spiral, the land that
crushes dreams, the dying youth, the assaulted
women who march, silently, over their wounds,
forever covering their words under the veil
of shame generated by a supposedly modern
society.

To young people in precarious neighborhoods
like City of God, the governments and candidates
for power give weapons and a few rations of
rice to assert their dishonest plans disguised
as democracy. Enlisted for the same reasons,
but not by the same people, these kids excel at
fighting, and in the process, choose in the city
as they see fit, bodies to be slaughtered, breaths
to be extinguished, souls they send to heaven
without a return ticket. Between fear and
precariousness, despair is invited. Governments
succeed each other, guns continue to sing, there's
never rice for all the mouths, life resembles
more than ever the trash that surrounds us, the
survivors are the violent flies that manage to fly
over it.

Here, there's the human scent that we'd like
so much to share and the smell of cockroaches
who asphyxiate our words. Chaos during the

day, dawn stuck in the sharp-edged song of the nights, raw barbed wire taming the dermis of our hopes. We're bodies mixed up in the scraps of life, voices in need of a sweet song, we're this neighborhood, an ass waiting to be wiped…

Prison. Here, my neighborhood. Here, the strange City of God, where my dreams heat up too far from my beloved flesh, who must be opening her blouse to the worldly winds of New York. Here, this fertile perimeter to my desolation. Human breath no longer has the smoothness of flapping wings. Here, prison of life's momentums. There's nothing to see in our walls but a frozen horizon. Disoriented dreams that can't manage to reform the takeoff point. Season eclipsed in the threads of time. The turmoil of the century overwhelms us, but our actions are always reduced to punctuating inertia. Space will tell you about the heaviness of the void.

For lack of caresses, our bodies indulge in the language of the rubble. Our footsteps fade in the lands of life, leaving the dust to conjugate. At the call of everyday life, there are no words to describe the adventures of the quest for survival. Between the need to conquer a piece of life, to see a better tomorrow and the invasion of filth, the wall of social inequalities erected in front of us, between the hope of living differently and the margin that is imposed on us to live, the eternal cycle of contempt, there must be a need to die. We're beings in agony, like eyes in the grip of a dust storm.

Here, everything is glory for nothing, hallelujah for shit...

've been living here for a while now, deep in this rotten neighborhood, in this slum that has no shortage of peers nearby. A dilapidated hut to rust our bodies throughout the days. Small concrete tower that tries to support a sheet of metal as best as possible. Two rooms, or rather just the perspective, with this curtain stretched in the middle. A window, the only one, opens onto a corridor. It's condemned by an opaque fabric that is lifted only when a strange noise from outside calls on us. If this opening were at the other end of the house, where the outhouses are, we'd really be in deep shit. They relieve a dozen asses, and the odor stinks like nothing else.

*T*he important thing is that we've got a place to live, we've got a door through which to enter and exit. Something to cram into while waiting to get out of the red block and enter into existence, the real one. An address, even if we're short of landmarks in the meanders of life.

Not quite alive, but we're here, under this
roof that witnesses the parade of our actions, our
failed acts, our easy sorrows and our difficult
pleasures. Face against the wall. Back against
the wall. Hands free their dirt by imposing it on
the walls. Critters get crushed against the wall
where their cadavers hope in vain for a funeral
for a very long time. A body—most often a child
or woman—huddles against the walls to cushion
a beating. Hands separating the head from the
wall, someone cries. Palms struggling against
the wall, someone welcomes another's cock from
behind. The walls thus bear witness to so many
passages. The walls wield the rich memory of a
million grips.

Few dishes. Perhaps because it's difficult to
fill them. Two large basins sit in a corner of
the room, when they aren't competing to rid the
clothes of human traces. A few chairs, which will
soon succumb due to accommodating behinds,
encircle an old table that seems to stumble but
somehow resists. It stands up against time, all
those years of watching an arsenal of guns being
cleaned. All those years of watching bodies
mingling in the inferno of sex. All those years

of watching bottles emptying out and a woman being filled up.

There are three of us here. But we never count each other around the table. In the same small box, but to each their own territory. Finally me, caught between thousands of worlds, I only try to shape my own. Yet we're supposed to do common work in this room, to give life to this perishing roof.

There's the fan that doesn't work but which completes the decor. There's the noise of the neighborhood that washes up here, giving meaning to our silences. The taste of emptiness. The heat and the mosquitoes. And the kingdom of shabby clothes, where three human shadows reign: Papa, Orange Blossom, and me. No mirror, perhaps to better avoid our faces, to better miss ourselves. That doesn't prevent Papa from being perpetually tormented by his reflection. He only needs to rest for a second to see his double invade him, to let go for a moment for another spirit to overwhelm him. The one he wanted to be, the man without the criminal hand. His other. The part he never got to graft. The Angel of Metal, in his odyssey of blood, doesn't give a shit about the human that Papa might've been. If he was to be the one to shape the latter, well, let's say he only managed to draw the kid's index finger in the shape of a trigger. Young Papa, doomed to kill since then.

*T*he water does its thing in a public fountain five hundred meters from here, letting a heap of containers moan for hours before it enters them. Sometimes you have the choice to pay for it at a hell of a price from a neighbor who was able to fill enough buckets. Too bad for our bodies, we don't always want to wash when we've got to do it out in the open. Too bad for our thirsts, our lives have dragged on for ages under the embrace of deserts.

*Y*ou could say that here, we're alone in the great night.

I'm a derelict ridden by loneliness in this dark valley where I'm writing an endless letter to my beloved.

In the light of things, we shouldn't have lived for filth, entrusted our existence to the flowers of shit. I often wonder where this logic of putting off the essential of the moment until tomorrow comes from. No answer, especially since I never dare to ask the question. Orange Blossom and Papa prefer to make a hard time surviving today, to invest their income in future projects that life may not even let them realize. It's idiocy, I'd say. A bit like those Christians who have nothing against the suffering and the excesses of the world, so convinced that they'll soon—a "soon" that is becoming increasingly longer—get to enjoy an unprecedented well-being in a place unknown by human sense, a place of unclear existence, a paradise whose description betrays the truth: a certain heaven where people will end up as robots, condemned to join hands and glorify a pope more despotic than the one on earth.

*O*range Blossom's job is to raise the bar for pleasure in order to optimize her profit.

She doesn't do charity work, and her body brings
in a good amount. The Divine, the Lord of the
Groin, and the Politician whose ass is made for
every chair, three regular customers for a total
of eleven thousand gourdes per month. Not to
mention the performance bonuses that go beyond
what's usual for fuckers. An ounce for the needs
of the house. A good portion for alcohol and
something to smoke. And all the rest to save. She
cherishes the idea that one day she'll gather her
small fortune and move to Amsterdam to become
a famous performer of sexual arousal, fucking
high-end. Pretty soon. Because she feels that her
body has only a decade of good work left.

*P*apa is the highest paid of the Angel of
Metal's soldiers. A fairly fat income that
is renewed with each raid, and that increases
with the size of the hunt and the talent devoted.
Licensed killer and well versed in many other
crimes, the man executes the designs of his leader
with wonder. And victims, that's not what's
missing in the city when death dogs of his caliber
get down to business. Kidnappings, gun sales,
hacks, drug trafficking, impossible missions,
commissioned killings, robberies, and other work

on behalf of the Angel of Metal. The combined percentages net him one hell of a fortune. Not to mention what he pockets with the dirty tasks that he makes up for himself, unbeknownst to his boss.

A very small slice is allocated to us. Enough to pay one of the local schools for my education, which I don't even take the time to really receive, so taken am I by the school of life. Enough to contribute scantily to feed the house. And he only knows how to spend to give flesh to his dream, his dream of a quiet and lonely tomorrow. All Papa wants to do with his money, without giving it to anyone, is build a superb villa in an area quite secluded from the main streets, so as to escape the crowd of looks. A place from which to better rule the city. Far from the human tide. A villa to accompany his solitude. Somewhere where he'll be able feel his peace.

And me? *You'll be…*

If I had the money, me, I'd be sailing in the lower abdomen of the sky right now, I'd be tearing the clouds apart to join my fairy on the other side of America. If I had some of this metal, of this paper worthy of time in these so-called United States, right now I'd be in New York, in the arms of my moon.

As if the pain had decided to eat more than ever. In the deprived neighborhood of Martissant, it was a period when violence worked like a mule, pointing its arrows at all the heavenly bodies of life. A hoarse song followed, irretrievably red, in which the days couldn't melt away without sullying the ears with the chorus of bullets, without raining dead bodies and thereby ruffling all sunshine of germinating hope. The neighborhood sky had folded, had paled in the image of the faces that inhabited it, these ghosts guilty of coming to scrape the strings of existence. Bouquets of pain, like frail stories colliding against rocks. So many horrible landscapes, the eyes came to lose all ability to contemplate. So many barbwire surfaces, the bodies couldn't embrace the supple ways of thinking. In vain, time killed itself to look beautiful, but a bitter taste skinned all horizons to settle on the lips of life.

It often happened that people, returning home to the murmur of twilight, were robbed of the miserable coins earned at the cost of sweat thrown in the unsanitary Croix-des-Bossales market. A man could get killed if word got around that he'd visited the inner thighs of a girl on which a thug was forming a sexual fantasy. It was by no means rare to open your door in the early morning to find a lifeless body lying in a bath of fresh blood. It happened that a child leaving school came across a shoot-out, had to let himself be snatched by a man to curl up in his shop and only come out the next day, once the sobbing of guns had stopped, to reunite with his parents, who, in the depths of anxiety, were preparing to brave the street to find their son or at least his body abandoned by breath.

As for the cops, they were, as always in this country, busy not honoring their job: imposing their own taxes on drivers to prevent them from having to pay official fines, clubbing people who, for lack of anything better, displayed their small shop, their little survival boat on the sidewalks, bothering guys by asking them to prove that they weren't thugs despite their braids or their tattoos, beating up students or workers who occupied the streets to demand their right to live better. The cops were very motivated for this part of the catalog of their missions, they loved to perform their savageness, to confirm their reputation as executioners in front of the journalists' cameras. Their faces were going to end up as the heroes in the media. They received hazard pay from the government for helping to maintain order.

The police didn't care to bring to an end this deadly symphony that harassed Martissant. Only once, a few policemen, who wanted to shock the population, had descended in the hope of stopping or at least mitigating a disastrous situation, and in the process lost their lives. The people of the country where no one has ever been buried with their hat on had made short work of their breaths.

In such an atmosphere, the school of crime could only see its numbers swell. The monstrosity had enlarged its territories. Black roses grew around all the edges. The game was unstoppable. To catch this skinned sky, take up arms to be part of those who decided the color of life in the city, or risk becoming their guinea pig, to survive while waiting for the passport to infinite dust: one way or another, you had to choose to save your skin from the grim grip, find an alternative to keep your veins away from the field of blades.

his was the dark valley having seen its childhood sink.

He lived with his mother and had no one else to cling to, no other arms to throw himself into to soften the assaults of life. She also acted as a father, if he needed one. For, early in her youth, a scumbag hadn't bothered to turn around—sorry, apparently he hadn't come for that, had been content to cum before getting the hell out—and so hadn't turned around after sowing a burst of sperm deep inside her without her permission.

He had a name that meant nothing until that night when everything was going to change, that night when he was going to have to experience the improbable. What meaning does a name have around here if the street doesn't give you one? The Angel of Metal, he was then baptized. Valiant name immortalized in the aftermath on his right bicep. Small man transformed into a dragon one evening when it had become impossible for him to live in his usual skin, after having been forced to witness an event of unprecedented gravity: his mother being beaten up and then killed by bandits upset to have found too little while robbing her purse.

The blast of the gun on the woman's temple ravaged his memory. Unable to sweep away this image, he tried to reconstruct his mother's smile, the lack of which was already too heavy. A smile that, despite the poor glimmer of the seasons, could be as intact as that of a family in a summer vacation photograph. He'd drained so much water from his eyes, but to break the lines of his grief, even the seas had proved insufficient. Chaos had taken control of the scene from his mind. At the height of his fifteen years, the kid had inflicted a lot of pain on himself to try in vain not to become the one that the street was going to, knowingly, validate right away: the Angel of Metal. He'd been knocked out by sleep that night. The next morning, he'd followed the call to the letter by confiding in the street, opening the arteries of a neighborhood that didn't need to be asked to give him the keys for his criminal life.

Two days hadn't passed before the Angel of Metal was in the truth of his prophecy, had already conquered the profession of his life… or perhaps his death. It was too late for his relatives to pull from the red zone this boy who'd marked his mother's funeral by his absence.

———

he noise, the violence, the fury, the anguish, the destitution, the flight, the despair, the tears, the horror, the abyss, the blood, the terror, the death, and the cries, all misfortunes had cracked the ceiling. A few years had passed, bequeathing bits of silence to the heart of the once too-tumultuous region. Death had ended up reaping a significant harvest of human heads. Among the inhabitants of Martissant, some had ceased to live there, had gone to other neighborhoods to deposit what remained of their lives. Others, having forced things to save the necessary amount, had cut through the clouds in large metallic birds to go harvest a better life off the island. The remaining were made up of a small group of beings overcome by emptiness and desolation.

You'll be... You'll be alone.
You'll be alone in the great night.

t twenty, the Angel of Metal was resolved to abandon this land that was tired of its heels, to settle in the City of God. Coincidence or calculation, it fell exactly on the day when the former head of the city had just disappeared.

According to the legend of the mouth that gives
and the ear that receives, the latter had all on
his own shot a bullet into his brain with his
adored Beretta, over some story about a baby
that his woman was fabricating while laid-up in
a hospital bed...

Dear Moon,

*I remember the day that saw our bodies light
up in the toilets of the church while a saddened
crowd addressed a requiem to your father. We
were two beings united in one breath. We were,
you and I, one blood flow and the memory of the
same country, a bullet and a body in the night
of Port-au-Prince. Through your prisms, I've
known the curves of the great dream and the
path of human magic. Beyond our erasures, I've
experienced the gesture of the only truth worthy
of this name: walking in the other.*

*And arrives the time of rubble, the reign
of ashes: fallen, our inner cities; collapsed, the
towers of our antics. There's the implacable
invasion of this distance that places our hearts
in the most total inertia. The fire speaks, the
smoke traverses, there remains in my soul this
icy silence when one Thursday you cling to the
wounded roads of America, when one day you
end up leaving the heaviness of your back in the
weak lines of my eyes. From now on so many
hills rise between us, so many ruins thrown*

between our stares. The void has its song in the
scum of distance.

I see a city dying out in your flight,
my bohemian language and the steps of my
wandering crumble in the shadow of your
skin. And I lose all desire to roam. And I ruin
myself searching for the meanders of your
azure. Was it not here, however, that the star
had blossomed, was it not here that this chorus
had been formed? I remember your look, your
smile, and our hands linked to tell the evidence
of a sky that revokes the clouds, and I remember
that cold day of the requiem to your father and
of our paths of fire in the walls of these church
toilets, of our saliva trafficking, which the angels
must've wanted to make eternal…Now you're
gone, and I see all the alchemy settling in your
body. I see the seasons come and go, all encrusted
in bile, they mourn the absence of your mouth, of
your body. Me, metal with short hands, I watch
the light flow into the distance.

T*he **Angel*** of Metal is a highway robber, and he owes his reputation to the fact that he never misses a target, never wastes a single cartridge, thus honoring his name to perfection. He's not the type of guy who backs down from any act, no matter the degree of madness and cruelty it might require. He's always ready to do anything to prove, if only to himself, that he doesn't belong in the common field of mortals. Where there's a lack of power, one doesn't hesitate to give him some. And that can sometimes go beyond the level of the trigger and take on the metaphysical. For example, ever since he arrived in City of God, people haven't stopped comparing him to the former head of the district, because the latter had been just as powerful; the legend of the mouth that gives and the ear that receives goes so far as to say that he's his reincarnation. The absents, they say, are always wrong; this guy shouldn't have left, so that today we could really measure his strength against that of the current leader. The predecessor of the Angel of Metal, to escape a child he didn't want—

without really knowing why exactly—offered his head to a Beretta in the public square on the day of the birth, and an hour later we saw his presumed corpse leave, smoked, lost to the horizon. Like everyone else, the mother has undoubtedly heard the story, but no need to count on her for any investigation, because she doesn't wish, has never wished, to get involved in the affairs of the dead. *If your father were here . . .* that's all she can whip out when she talks to her child, despite the rumors in the crowd. Everything is as true as it's false in this country, it depends on the mouth that gives, it depends on the ear that receives. This man, did he really exist, did he really commit suicide, did he really come back to live in the body of the Angel of Metal? The legend mutates over the days but no one knows how to establish a link with any truth.

The Angel of Metal doesn't care about this strange story featuring him, he has nothing to lose. On the contrary, this kind of thing gives him an even more fearsome image in the neighborhood. When he hears that he's the reincarnation of someone else, he mockingly asks what human could storm his body without him killing it . . .

Whatever. His world is about dropping bodies from the tree of breath. Capable of anything, so no need to say how often the Angel of Metal is called on to finish dirty jobs.

A certain young bourgeois is arrested by the police because he smokes marijuana in his car while belting out David Guetta tunes to show the girls accompanying him that he's cool. It costs him two days in police custody; after his release, his father comes to ask that the cop be taught a fatal lesson.

The owner of a major company arrives—he calls beforehand, to warn, otherwise he risks being misunderstood by the chief's soldiers for tearing up the belly of the village with his late-model Toyota—he asks that his competitor's son be kidnapped and that the ransom demanded be so high that the man will only consider the bankruptcy of his business.

A rather mediocre legislative candidate comes to negotiate votes.

A kid wants to get a gun, a real one. Come on, it's free for kids!

Ministers and chief executives always have scores to settle, someone to quiet definitively. When the official armored vehicles plow through the district, don't believe that they've come to feel sorry for our fate. The president himself can land here when he wants to best ensure the smooth operation of a bloody case.

The Angel of Metal thus has a rain of visits. Because for all the bloody wishes, he always has an answer.

No veil on the gashes.

No shroud on the wounds, even
the ripe ones.

A strange feeling consumes me. Shells burst
in my throat. I come to spout words. I speak.
And I speak. Alone in my night, I aspire to
defeat something that haunts me, a phrase
devoted to sewing me a terrifying destiny. *You'll
be…*

Ever since my love crumbled, a sad song lies
along my body.

I talk to myself and my words reach Silence,
this absence that torments me, I speak and it's
my cry, a supreme breath that keeps me standing
in my rage, like liberating music. There you go,
I talk to myself like this, in a vacuum. Without
pretense to offer cries to the virgin voices of
the world. Without pretense of scourged ink
on the intact page. It's so light and perhaps
totally insignificant to speak in the absence.
But there's nothing precious in a word that'd be
made only to fill: to fill ears, to fill pages, to fill
other mouths, other voices. Words like to throw
themselves into the void, so the important thing

is to create the void and let them flow. Every mouth that speaks is a story, mine is nothing special. My life, a cargo of despair that I'm condemned to bear. If I speak, it's to clear my passage, to lighten my race. I talk to myself and I feel like I'm pushing my voice to bump into the sky to make stars fall on my face.

You'll be... You'll be alone.

You'll be alone in the night. You'll be alone in the great night.

Here I am, a tale of the abyss in search of an asylum at the end of the letters. A saying lives in me like a clot of blood helping me to die, to die in silence, in the broken echo of lightning. I spit, but the words have nowhere to fall. My voice becomes a symphony of the tomb, a song capable of cradling the Sahara. Life apprehends the pallor at the sight of my face. Here I am, a mutilated flower seeking refuge in the dark land. And by this overflowing stream of words, a flurry of letters exploding the limits of my language, what have I to spit? An alphabet of volcanoes, red words, words wounded by the fire of violence.

I feel my heart slowly capsizing towards nothingness. It's a cigarette that comes to lift me up. I take a puff and in no time I empty out a carton. I've been smoking for some time, and

from the beginning I felt that it was an eternal
gesture, that this pact between two fingers
and lips to supply clouds to the horizon was
an infinite path. One thing is clear: one puff
can't solve the problem of a thirsty lung that
didn't know it was thirsty until it experienced
the tenderness of a first puff. The sensation one
experiences when pressing one's lips on a joint
or a cigarette has no other outcome than to be
prolonged eternally. The doctors may shout
that carcinogenic fate makes a killing among
smokers, but nothing stops the smoke, nothing
can stop it, it insists and ends up crossing the wall
of arguments with the greatest ease. Smoking
is an eternity. And that's why when you quit
smoking, or, better, when you think you've quit
smoking, there's a terrible loss, an immense
emptiness that only the grace of a fresh puff can
stop. Never will we be able to count on a single
cigarette to kill this craving, whose only virtue is
to go through life itself.

irearms of all kinds are spread out on an old table; a basin dirty like the rest of the place is filled with banknotes, another with bullets; there are also telephones and computers, an old mattress on the floor, bottles of beer, cigarette butts on the ground, and at the entrance a guard holding a long gun. It's dark and very hot. For those who aren't used to this particular kind of palace, it's hard to breathe. I'm in the room with air conditioning, it's the Angel of Metal's office. I'm here to deliver a package to him from Papa. He makes me wait, the time to meet a client, so that he can check it.

The boss flaunts such a tight face that I wonder how the man will be able to negotiate with him. The Angel of Metal would love to open the book of praises of his employees, to scroll through their track record pinned with honorable mentions, to brag about the singular qualities of bestiality of the eminent Papa, for example, to tell how such a protégé is wedged in the suspension of human breath and also impervious to pity, capable of the worst in matters of horror.

But the guest is ahead of him from the start.
The client weighs enough on the scale to ask
for what he wants. A check for five hundred
thousand gourdes won't be worth a discussion. I
didn't come to see you to ask for someone else, I
didn't come to borrow the boss's footsteps to go
towards his soldiers, it's your hand that I want
to give shape to my wish. The Minister of Social
Affairs takes care to entrust the file on the target
to be killed, then dries his voice, having nothing
else to add to make himself understood: he wants
to eliminate this man who threatens to take his
position, if we're to believe the recurrence of his
name during the Council of Ministers.

The card is thrown, the boss sets to work,
searches for ideas to get the job done with
elegance, soon finds the best one, and calms
down. He smiles thinking about it, regrets
having to wait for the night to vanish to go and
wipe out his new prey. He starts to get bored,
sets out to kill time by caressing the only thing
he believes deserves his trust and respect, the
only thing he takes for a true companion: a 9 mm
on which he recently engraved his initials.

He seems to forget me, which is why I now
hand him the bag. He checks that it's the right
goods, then gives me back a piece of paper that I
must've forgotten next to the package, asking me

if I'm writing letters to a boyfriend. I tell him no, it's not a boyfriend...

The Angel of Metal returns to his passion, he caresses his weapon with the attention and skill that he's known for. As always, he's ready to do anything to defend his title, doesn't want to sully his bloodthirsty reputation and so must get this right, can't disappoint this minister newly subscribed to the chain of monsters...

Dear Moon (so declared by my mouth),
It's the whole earth that I'm tearing, the whole
horizon that I'm stirring, that I question, it's
the whole sky that I'm shattering, to fish out
your face. O dear moon—thus proclaimed by
my mouth, my mouth adorned with light since
its stroll on your body—I want you in my arms
and in my inner lines, I want you on my path.

You came with the day under your wings,
that's all you passed on to me, and here I'm
writing to you, assisted by the sun, no doubt
living off your sap. You came via the hills
of tenderness, and your life by those of your
breasts, O daughter of the late, I invoke you, lost
in the bush of emptiness, I call your eyes, the
night surrounds me, I need your eyes to slap it to
death. I need to continue our gestures. I miss y

Syllable, then tremor.
Word, then emptiness.
Sentence, then deletion.
Letter, then paper in pieces.
Struggling to make some piece of light.
It limps, it stumbles and breaks.

A veil on the breach.

As if the night was focused on undoing the knots of the dream that I've been trying for a long time to put down on paper. Hours go by where I shake the sky of the verb, still unable to capture stars. I feel the night striking on my head with all its forces, it splashes on the sheet— refuge of barely a few words—lowers the pen and, unstoppable, comes to paint my eyes in its image.

The sound that lifts my chest is gray. I quit thinking about my love and lie on the rug right beside me. I hear Morpheus's boots scamper behind me, turmoils, winds in my sail, push me away and prevent him from catching me. This lasts a few good minutes. But here is my exhausted body, and my spirit surrenders to the sound of unconsciousness.

Oh how much this day was hoped for! We planned everything for a few weeks. The papers are now ready. I've got a passport and a visa, and all the other gibberish that the countries with depressed humanity require from hearts that are just waiting to beat on what they consider to be their soil. The clock strikes and here I'm finally on my way to my point of hope. I'm moving towards my beloved, sailing towards my moon. In the airport, I observe sad departures, hugs and kisses that'd like to be endless. These pains ring inside me and give me a rage that makes me want to knock the heads off the immigration officers, these apostles of boredom on a mission for birds deprived of wings because of a bad passport. To disperse these misfortunes from my head, I think about my heart, which will soon open. In a few hours, the big reunion. New York is going to burst into flames.

On the plane, children cry for attention, drool, vomit when that isn't enough; their parents talk too loudly to appease them; men keep needing to pee, getting blocked by old

women who parade with the same slowness as
their index fingers inside their nostrils; young
high schoolers eat peanut butter, the smell
is throwing my nose out of whack; the flight
attendants replay their years-old choreography;
they talk like a pair of scissors, each of their
sentences seems to be a tribute to symmetry; the
words "seat belt" are the greatest wealth of their
vocabulary; I'd like them to stop taking us for
babies...

I wake up with a jolt from this dreadful
journey. Night has given me an incredible
nightmare. Catching my breath with difficulty,
I regret not having remained trapped there
because I know that my thirst to find my moon
would've helped me to hold out until the end.
But shit, nothing is possible. I make a ship out of
anger.

At this precise moment, I'd like to invite
dawn to perch on my head to reveal to my eyes
the face of my lover and introduce my being
into an asylum outside of the shadows. But the
night continues, and what remains for me is
a carnal symphony interrupted sometimes by
Papa's voice—Oh yeah, oh yeah, is that good?—
sometimes by mom's—Yes, yes, go ahead, hit
me, oh yes, that's good. And I hear blows, and

I hear screams… Puzzled, I feel like I've fallen into a new nightmare. I let my head rest on the threshold of silence, summoning a last drop of sleep.

*A*t daybreak, the streets are tackling a new matter. The news has already won everyone's lips: the supreme leader has just left. This inevitably means the coming of bloodshed. The air reeks of danger, death rising in the nostrils, we think of the potential flow of corpses, everyone rushes to vacate the premises. Even some of his soldiers, unaware of his plan, seek shelter far from his path. They remember the one who the commander shot down on the main road of the city, almost a year ago, because the latter had orchestrated a very profitable robbery without his knowledge.

*W*e could well say that the Angel of Metal's movements punctuate the clock, he proceeds by measuring the time he has left to act, he's thirsty to reiterate his performance at the trigger. It's been a few days since he's been out, that he has stayed in his kingdom, the room with air conditioning, and that he has sent the others on a mission. He has finally decided to take to the streets today and doesn't intend to return empty-handed. Neighborhood fences can only see him from behind now. Here is Papa picking him up on the back of a motorcycle: they're pushing towards Turgeau, towards the Social Assistance Fund, where their next victim earns a staggering salary for a management position without really working. It's not very far, the watch is calm, it ticks just right, it's going to be on the dot, the office is waiting for ten o'clock to open. The target will show up at the right time, and will fall into the arms of the wrong man.

They're only forty meters away now. The Angel of Metal recognizes the car of the man to be killed, the color, make, and license plate. He asks Papa to stop and wait for him here, he walks alone towards the vehicle which he sees bouncing on the spot… He asks that the door be opened for him, threatening to discharge his weapon. He can't believe his eyes. The ultimate slap in the face… A half-naked woman, whose face he recognizes well—and perhaps the body too, if we're to believe the legend of

the mouth that gives and the ear that receives—
exits the car in a sweat, her poorly put on thong
carries aloud the message of a body that had just
returned from another body.

The wanted man stays in the car, he curls into
a shell, thinks of lowering his eyes but remains
vigilant, he visualizes the brittle smile of his
executioner asking him to choose between dying
and dying, imagines the shrillness of the window
and his blood on the cushion, measures the
distance to the steering wheel to try to escape.
Looking taken aback, watching the Angel of
Metal walk away with the woman, he thinks
about his corrupt career, of the opportunities to
serve his country denied by his greed, and the
sound of guilt resonates within him. What have
I done not to die, what do they have to leave
without shooting me?

The killer, meanwhile, is no longer interested
in the man in the car, he has forgotten his
target for a more important matter to deal with.
He raises his voice: insults launched against
the woman of his best soldier, criticizing her for
being too indiscreet and so clumsy in choosing

her client. How could you dare come and operate here? In front of a state office, in the middle of the day, in the middle of the street, under the eyes of the entire republic… It's like you don't think. On top of that, with such a bastard!

The leader turns his head and now realizes that his target has fled in the car, which angers him even more. He takes out his rage against the woman. You don't deserve to live, bitch! The Angel of Metal slaps her and pushes her towards Papa. He now waits, as a matter of course, for him to pull the trigger, for him to kill her. Papa, who until then had been buried in his silence, pretends to acquiesce and prepares for the execution, doesn't give the time to his second voice to speak, kills the words of his interior light that would have surely considered the rights of the individual to use their body as they please, that would have rung the bell, raised the hand for justice and dignity, for human rights, for the rights of women.

While a hymn of tears devours his heart, he pulls the trigger to save his reputation in the eyes of his leader. Three gunshots follow each other in tempo. Orange Blossom embraces the ground.

Ravaged on the inside, Papa loses himself for a few seconds in the body quenching the asphalt with a red squirt. Deep down, he resents the

Angel of Metal for coercing him into killing his woman, but doesn't dare express that feeling. This state of affairs reinforces an idea that he has been mulling over for a long time: dethroning his leader.

He grinds his teeth before starting the bike…

*A**n hour after* the tragedy, the news reaches City of God and devastates me like matches in the eyes, transforms me into this kind of disarmed concrete where bombs run after their echo. A big piece of me disappears, like a fist comes undone in a fight. And I've got nothing but emptiness to lick. it's not hugs that life takes away from me but a body, a being, that I'll no longer see loving me, even in silence.

You'll be… You'll be alone.
You'll be alone in the night.

I pile up screams that slap my throat. Trapped by a curtain of tears, they transform into sobs. The drunkenness of an atrocious memory announces itself on the line of my glass, the din of anguish knocks at my door. The tragic promise of infinite traces on paper. I weep for my mother, fire on my skin, the pain shatters from outside, but there are also a thousand reasons to cry, so many other tears squeezed by stories, so many other waves locked in repressed stories. There's my mother, or rather the story she carries, the arms of my grandparents that

she didn't know as a cradle. Precariousness
never allowed them to skip town, but I still don't
understand why their baby ended up on a pile
of trash. If this man hadn't discovered it before
the animals and taken her to grow up in his
orphanage, my mother would've been dust for a
long time and I wouldn't have been born into this
world.

It's going to be on the radio, through a
rather pale voice, fabricated to the second
for the painful circumstances, the supposedly
sincere sympathies and the condolences devoid
of any emotion. This moment that will push
most listeners to change stations. It'll be in the
newspaper, in the little corner of a page that few
people will want to read. A note formulated in
advance in which the deceased is renamed and
the testimony detailing the conditions of their
fall is added. An alert addressed to the relatives
of the victim, who had to suspend her striptease
to appreciate the brutal touch of a bullet on
the temple. A call to the family of the woman
found drowned in her blood, with a crooked
thong. A call to claim the possibly already frozen
body in a morgue, under the perverse eye of

the undertakers, those sneaky folks who don't hesitate to use the dead to live...

Behind the scenes of the neighborhood, everyone is talking about the event. The trumpet of life has registered a final sound for the lady. She's dead, the woman of the off-peak hours, the woman who never has anything to add after saying hello, not even a smile. She's dead, the passerby of the day whose eyes housed the friction of the night. Yet no one dares to talk to Papa about it directly, we know he doesn't give a damn about the dead. For him it's silly to have to invest in a body divorced from breath, to be in a hurry to find it a new home, to pay an overwhelming amount of money to buy it chic clothes and a piece of furniture that wants to look beautiful. There's no point in exhausting a piece of life for a cadaver, he says. Let it rot on its own and get as far away from its stench as you can.

I run to the scene of the crime to try to see my mother's face one last time—I've always felt

a tenderness buried under that difficult face,
which must be soft now that it's reached the
afterlife. I hold back my tears so as not to draw
a crowd around me. A man nearby tells me that
a funeral home has just left with the body—he
tells me where to find it, a few hundred meters
from here. I arrive at the morgue, three women
are standing at the entrance and are about
to close the gate. Behind glasses dark like a
hearse, their faces resemble the oldest tomb
in the cemetery of Port-au-Prince. I can't tell
if they're silent in order to welcome me and
listen to me, or if they're going to bite me like
the dead, if they're going to squeeze my neck
like they do to people who hang around on
the edges between life and death and who are
unfortunate enough to find themselves here. I
dare to speak to them. Little girl, we're sorry,
laments one of them, not wanting to exaggerate,
your mother wasn't *simple*, we've got the proof.
You know, she stirred things up around here,
and besides, we shouldn't be talking to you,
we've got to wonder what trouble you came
to assign us. A tigress's daughter is a tigress,
isn't that what they say? You know what, little
girl, we've been here twenty years doing what
others are afraid to, and criticize when our
only concern is to make sure they don't end up

like rotting flesh, for twenty years we've been helping bodies fight the stench, death is our thing, it's in our skin, to each his own passion, yes, it's also to earn a living but it's first out of love that we do it. If there's one thing we look forward to, it's to please cadavers, take care of them as they should be, so that they don't go knocking on heaven's door with a dirty ass. We've been doing this for twenty years and are a reference in the field, it's like we were born to work in death's domain, we've seen it all, trade unionists killed by young people with illegal weapons provided by the government, women clubbed to death by their partners in the middle of the street, children killed because their parents didn't have enough to pay their captors, bystanders of the bicentenary, rebellious students, workers who wanted to unionize, guys with dreadlocks who did nothing but find themselves in front of the police, pedestrians who lived in a city with no crosswalks, drivers who drove on a road without traffic codes in a country where the only traffic violation is that of not bribing the cop who stops you, people who tried to live or think outside heterosexual society, people who believed they could cultivate dignity in the political field, patients who for the lack of structure waited too long in front of Hôpital Général, in short, all kinds of corpses have paraded around here. They enter through this door and never—go ask them if you want—leave by their own free will, never leave again except to go fatten Baron Samedi's big family, never have we had such a case here. Your mother, in fact, is the very first to make us question our work. What will the city say now? That we're incompetent, that we can't handle the dead? Honestly, your mom is really crazy for pulling this trick over on us! We fought a lot for her, if our paramedic was here, he'd tell you what we went through, how he had to fight with staff from other morgues to get her. When the body arrived, we thought it was a real one and we were so happy to welcome it, it's our job, we treat the dead to live, as I just told you, we immediately got to work on your mother's body, not without an ounce of pleasure. She had breasts that could take down the sky, perfect hips, legs that seemed not to lack flexibility when they had to open, basically, a body that deserved more than our expertise. We cleaned her up really well, and when the job was done, we just went outside to get some fresh air when a strong wind blew through the building. We're telling you, you weren't there, little girl. You had to live this moment. A wind so strong that

it sounded like all the cyclones of the world had
gathered here, as if the god that the legend of
the mouth that gives and the ear that receives
had enthroned beyond the clouds had let out a
big fart to put an end to this land that is said
to be his work. We just had time to hold on to
this wrought iron. Everything was going in
all directions: chairs were bumping against
the ceiling, desks were overturning, windows
were breaking, coffins were flying and landing
on our heads, the place was shaking like the
president's head shakes when the people go
out into the streets to shout their unhappiness.
This apocalypse lasted no more than fifteen
seconds, but was enough to bring us down.
Our bodies in sweat, we were getting ready to
face the damage, were already thinking about
the nightmare of reorganizing the space, when
a total darkness seized the morgue. There, we
really flipped out, we said that's it, it's the end
of the world, ten seconds later the lights came
back on and everything went back to its place.
We couldn't believe our eyes, felt like we were
trapped in a bad dream. We then started to
check to see if it was real, if everything was
really still there and in its place. I called out
the name or the description of the corpses and
my colleagues took care of confirming their

presence, and that's when we noticed that
everyone was there except your mother. She got
us, you can't imagine what a mess she leaves us
in, she leaves without even spending an evening
with us...

A body that enters this room never comes
out, except to go to the cemetery. I swear to you,
we do everything to ensure that this principle
is respected... It's the first time that this type
of thing has happened to us. The legend of the
mouth that gives and the ear that receives says
that this phenomenon already happened once
in a neighborhood not far away, but it's the very
first time that we've seen such a mystery with
our own eyes. That's why we're closing. We'll be
the first to say it: you don't close a morgue in a
city like ours, where death works hard. But right
now, it's not possible, we've got to take control of
the situation before we're able to start working
again.

Go, push the gate, said the woman to her
colleagues. Goodbye, little girl, we've got to go.
Tonight, we're going to see Baron Samedi, he's
the guardian of all the villages of the dead in all
the cities of the world, perhaps he'll be able to tell
us more...

After listening, heartbroken, to this strange

story, I leave empty. There'll be no funeral, there'll be no final viewing, no last look. I'll mourn my mother between the passage of time and the silence of the walls.

You'll be alone in the great night. It's resonating.

he night stinks of boredom. Like a cadaver that hasn't yet taken its bath, it reeks of a failed dream. Struck against a trench of memories, I rob sleep with no luck. Sometimes night feels no pity, it lives within us to exile all peace and colonize the door of dreams. Boredom and emptiness take up residence in the mind. Thus there's no longer a dream that isn't woven with terror.

Here I am, bent under the blows, my forehead riddled with javelins of anguish, a wreckage brings my momentum tumbling down. The afterlife sings and sings again beyond my cries of flight, a heavy requiem that life hammers at the edge of my dreams, at the mouth of my days. I stir my sky in the dust, I drink from the river of vertigoes.

Since Silence's departure, I no longer have any limbs to crawl even in the wings of love, I can only roll in my dark mass of loneliness. The pulse of my heart is becoming this dry noise which rivals the deserts. The wonderless girl that I am carries a part of life that she doesn't really want to. I tremble under a burden of wet eyes

for the absence of a beloved that my body got
to know for a day. Even if my face sometimes
defies sadness, in truth I'm a soul struggling in
the darkness, a girl sailing alone, with hills in
mind and no ladder to climb them, like a taste of
falling for me that will take time to restore my
tattered clothes, mend my brokenness.

Silence isn't a point equal to others in the
horizon of my life. In her, the time of a trip to
the land of our bodies burned with desire, I felt
a heart where I could count my excess, the other
human with whom to carry my madness. A girl
that I love without being able to do anything else.
And now that that part of light has disappeared,
all that remains of me is a cellar of acrid words,
a flow of dirty sentences. Here is my moon, my
mirror-heart, getting away from me. And all that
remains of my inner song is a slew of metaphors
stuck in pale images, a pain-poem. Neither the
sand from all the seas, nor the wheat from China,
nor the human bodies taken for bomb sites in
Syria, nor the mouths in need of bread, nor the
refugees mutilated by the scalpel of borders, nor
the bullets that play music in Port-au-Prince, nor
the dead bodies of Titanyen, nothing in the world
can equal the damage handed down to my being
by the absence of my lover for a day…

The man is stuck in a shock-stunned
stone face. Dilapidated like an armchair
that describes absence. A nod to those
left flat broke by coke, his head reminds you of
those deforested mountains in the countryside
that wiggle between the whip of the sun and
the cannons of the rain. His face a cartography
of blank, worthy of a poorly cared-for corpse.
He's a pack of nothing that moves. However, his
gestures reveal the look of a man on the alert. He
embraces the street by smacking nonchalance.
His footsteps tell how much his thirst can swallow
a whole world. He doesn't seem to know what
to look for, though maybe he doesn't need
anything. His legs try their hand at a tumultuous
waltz, he walks with a passion capable of lifting
cathedrals. But deep down, nothing could
distinguish it from a tree with its canopy of
leaves in the snow.

　　Ruins for baggage. The man doesn't make
his weight from a story worthy of breaking the
record books, has nothing to feed the pages,
nothing to attempt a trace, even in the margins.
A proper politician of a rotten century in an

anonymous small country. No poem will want to say it, will be able to carry him, will be able to save this heap of silences, this body that had always denied its voice in the face of calls for help from the human choir.

He no doubt has just set fire to the fuse of a crowd that travels within him. Otherwise nothing would explain why he has started to run and scream like a loudspeaker claiming paternity of decibels. Nobody offers to stop it; we don't want to lower the curtain on this show. Each gesture a claw on the back of calm. The man throws the keys to his government car, the windows of which he has just broken at home to get rid of his rage. His gait gives the impression that he's only aiming to stir up the air. It's difficult to detect what's put him in this state. He quit the drugs. Since the scandal when a packet fell from his jacket in the middle of an official ceremony at the presidency, he told the Angel of Metal that he'd continue to give him money, but that he no longer wanted coke or cannabis.

The Politician whose ass is made for every chair seems to be sailing towards a new world: he draws his erasures, or rather his erasures draw him. Sometimes it embodies the strength of a fever, the ardor of vertigo. Sometimes he evokes the image of a drifting canoe, a young vagrant ravaged the day before by a rock concert.

The fugitive now has no more screams, or only lets his voice rest. He seems to savor a moment of loving silence.

*H*e slows down when he arrives at Champ-de-Mars, one must believe that some kind of fate pushed him to wind up here. If he gives himself a break during his pacing, it has nothing to do with needing to breathe. He's hot, but he still has so much breath to give in his new odyssey that he doesn't even notice it. His body doesn't care about his shortness of breath, regains its momentum in the slumber of the strides. Torn between the weakness of his wings and the burn of flight, the man does everything to divert his shadows and reach his peak.

*T*he Politician whose ass is made for every chair comes across a group of young people, seated, trading their emptiness for hazy words and sunless laughter. Without forcing the parentheses of tradition, it's clear that these young people are on the lookout for a scandal that is bound to explode in this public square. The man stops and talks to this guy who holds the sight of passersby hostage because he has no more room on his torso to accommodate tattoos, begs him to help him engrave the face of a woman who's just disappeared on his balls... He leaves without an answer, just has time to see his request turned into ridicule.

ike a sob at the forefront of a flood of tears, little by little his rhythm extinguishes his lucidity. In this streetlight that waits for the night to shine with its uselessness, he sees Orange Blossom. Suddenly, she leaps in a flash, temporarily embellishing each point in the space. The silhouette of the woman on the empty bench escapes before his eyes, he lets himself flutter with the expected energy of an actor, and having once again missed his prey, collapses against a concrete column towered by a hero—the hero's machete hoisted so it looks like he wants to restart the Revolution.

Right here, the Politician whose ass is made for every chair files his divorce from the protocol. The wild flanks of local politics have just lost an important figure, a face that made them look good in the press. The seats of public offices will no longer welcome this man and his suits that cost a fortune of the people's money... His jacket leaves to go cherish the asphalt, the tie prolongs the act of unkemptness, and the shirt cries out for its battered buttons. His body is certainly starting to feel good and quite nice in the arms of the air on this rare occasion. His belly doesn't seem to be ashamed of being a noticeable figure.

The man gets lost raising his depths, drowns himself touching his mountains, sews his delirium in a dark ray, loses his brilliance searching for himself in a blue sky strewn with cloudiness. He rushes towards the wall to catch his lover or at least the nomadic reflection that costs him this vicious nostalgia—perhaps he's just rediscovering a world hidden from our senses— he comes back towards the streetlight and turns around it, his shoes are hurting him, he gets rid of them, no, it's to facilitate the removal of his pants, which he begins to lower. Only underwear remains to prevent the absolute reign of nudity.

This growing crowd that was quick to surround him didn't expect the man to reject the idea of an audience so enthusiastic about what he accomplished without the pretension of putting on a show. The Politician whose ass is made for every chair grabs the streetlight in every possible way. A rough pilgrimage towards pleasure. While his flesh growls with pain, he smiles in the brittle movement of his hips, to think he was tearing the last shroud of pleasure. He cuts the erogenous paths in gestures no less ardent than vague. His penis gives itself vivid fractures, blood bathed in the glow of twilight pouring out all over, as if to give a better view of the gravity of the situation. The escapee's limb is bleeding like crazy...

The Politician whose ass is made for every chair picks up his clothes, gathers them into a disorderly bundle, which he rolls up in his jacket, then takes off before the crowd scatters, now filled with heterogeneous emotions. He resumes his walk, his mug submitted to the bottleneck of restless wandering.

eat that rises, sweat that descends, breath that alarms the air, voices that break the hesitation, cries that break free, fists that rise, rebellious song that is written, tires in flames, signs that tear the space, slogans that fire like machine guns: the street embraces the inferno of a crowd that'd come to spit out its need to live. We didn't expect to see so many people responding to the call for demonstrations by the small citizens' committee of Cité Paille. This is because their reasons for protest are the same as all the other precarious neighborhoods in the country: no access to drinking water and, over their few square kilometers, no fewer than five nongovernmental organizations have been carrying out projects for years at a cost of millions of dollars in the name of this problem. The crowd is huge, which goes to show how thirsty the population is for this moment. Everything can be read on these faces armed with rage and hope, from which rise voices that grow thicker and louder.

And here is the silence, the murderous silence that shows up. A procession of vultures sent by

Mister Commander in Chief to sow fear wherever
the noise of protest grows. I'm talking about these
cops, real executioners in hoods, I'm talking about
this herd of monsters called law enforcement
who come to cause trouble in the midst of people
standing up for a good cause. It brings to mind
the heads beaten, the unjust imprisonments, the
cries muffled by the bulldozers of a repressive
system, the fatal baton beatings, the murderous
bullets that don't miss their target, the voices
strangled for having dared to rise up, the angels
riddled with bullets for attempting to spread their
wings, the dead bodies piled up along the streets,
the piss that takes off in the face of struggle... The
cops have no love to share, or tenderness to sell,
they make hate speak and carry disgust in their
actions. As far as we can remember, we've never
seen such dirty ones. They show up with silence in
their tear gas canisters, they show up with *Shut the
fuck up* in their boots and *Shut your mouth, punk* at
the end of their guns.

The demonstrators were expecting this
scenario—which wouldn't be a first—and had
said to themselves that they were still going to
stick it out, stay on their feet, that they were
going to overcome the intimidation in any way
they could, that they weren't going to give up the
fight just like that. So they continue their song

of anger under the sun, some even add tires to burn, others throw stones at the police cars.

But it doesn't last long. Because the cops declare the situation grim and mark their entry into the game with gas jets. The human mass begins to disperse. A young worker falls, his face between his hands, his condition foreshadows an asphyxiation. A comrade puts a lemon peel under his nose and tries to support him to get him out of danger. Wind knocked out, and the crowd gradually rebuilds. Then comes the bounce back from the armed forces, with a first burst of bullets. And more tear gas.

*M*ore bullets and tear gas.
The crowd howls, the rifles go on...

A young girl watches her white jersey turn crimson, a friend shares his to tighten the path of the bullet that'd found refuge in her left breast. The girl cries while shouting insults, to say that she isn't losing the battle even if the worst is in the vicinity, even if misfortune has just unpacked its luggage in her bosom.

A journalist, heart pounding behind her lens, watches her cry over the spurt of blood, wants to cry with her but still thinks of the perfect shot it'll make for the next day's front page, swallows the alarm of the sobbing and continues her work.

A young man running at full speed is cut short in his tracks. A shot elicits an unimaginable cry of pain. The journalist doesn't miss the grimace on the face that comes with it. The charge seems to have hit the young militant in the penis. A red flood emerges terrifyingly from between his legs. Fallen right on the ground, he struggles in vain in the chorus of bloodshed.

Dressed in the uniform I usually wear, a group of schoolchildren gather on a sidewalk where something seems to be going on. According to the cry of one of them in front of the camera, a student has been shot in the stomach. She's in pain, and her classmates are crying, crying out for help, but no one comes to their aid. I try to monitor the situation carefully. The camera finally lands on the face of the victim, she looks like Silence. My heart cracks. As I jump over to the TV to take a closer look, I wake up sweating on the bed, no, on the rug. It pisses me off, it pisses me off, and it pisses me off. Cursed be this dream that couldn't bring me closer to my moon!

The Lord of the Groin, he, too, is struck by the news. He liked to drink from the erotic juice of this woman who's no longer, but who was so much to him. He could immediately get on his gray horse, raise a glass to the melancholy, stage his drama as needed to prove that he has just lost a loved one. But might as well rely on the gap of pleasure, he reasons. Might as well let off steam. In the name of the dead. For voluptuous affinity with life, sacred even in the face of death's disturbing orgasm. For the love of pleasure. What's life if you only taste the smallest part of a moment's breath?

There's no denying that he's a licensed pleasure-seeker. From head to toe, from the cutaneous envelope to the marrow via the veins, from the spirit of the body to the skin of the soul, a kind of epicurean always ready to break the folds of this life playing the schizophrenic bitch.

It all started with an intense anger against his country, a grudge against his city of stenches, black tears, murderous spit and sweat. Bloodless place where the perfume of the suns deteriorates between muddy lives and rain of corpses. It

all started when he realized that he shouldn't
fade away with the deadly shadows of Port-au-
Prince. The Lord of the Groin is angry with this
city of wounded skies, which carries the day
under the soles and the night on the arms, this
capital that dumps on the carpets of hope. City
of all heartbreaks, guinea pig of an infernal pain,
faults on fragile paths, rubble under the feet. He
resents this town, so he escapes into the caverns
of tobacco, sex, and booze.

A refresh of the face, a change of shirt, a
few phone calls, a slamming of the door,
and a few minutes later, he's on his way. As soon
as he enters the bar, he asks, shouting, that four
beers be brought for him and his friends in their
usual corner. The order is fulfilled very quickly,
knowing what the prolonged thirst of these
customers can cost.

Joy resonates from the bottles that are
uncapped. One of the guys loses himself in the
curves of the waitress who walks away from the
table, stares at her back until the last shadow
of the young girl's silhouette disappears: an
eye irreparably on the lookout for sex, which
doesn't even pay attention to the fact that the

young girl isn't an object. It's on now, a first swig to reconnect with the habit, a second to make sure that this beer is really good—the locals agree that it's the best in the world, even though they're afraid to taste another—and then a cigarette each.

Den of all human waves, where one gnaws away at the nights and their mission of sleep, this bar is a shore with a big heart, a sky where birds in need of branches in the savannah of daily life come to look for an elsewhere. Workers haunted by the torment of work, dragging the incendiary voice of the boss in their cervical carcasses even very far from the factory, the painful drudgery, and the wages of misery, students who are fed up with studying, wandering from all corners, subscribers to the bohemian channel, the unemployed, free electrons or prisoners of idleness, bodies overwhelmed by emptiness, young people on the lookout for new flesh, single people in search of the gaze of abandoned others, shards of hearts come to stick together on the horizon of a drink. Anyway, everyone forges a place for themselves here. Bazaar of all colors, of all heats.

This place is a bit like the second home of the Lord of the Groin. He comes regularly to scale the doors of his lungs, to fish rivers other than blood to irrigate his veins, to update his drunk status and then pull himself out of the window of illusions. And this evening, pinned around this table once again with his friends, he only seeks to pull out the weapon capable of countering the suffocating hints of sadness. On one side, a couple is sipping beer, exchanging light smiles as a precaution, so as not to get too close. On the other side, a young woman plunges her head into a glass of whiskey, vacillates between imprisonment and the burn of being quartered, expresses her loneliness by watching the passersby, who invite themselves joyfully into the beatings of the loudspeakers, scratches her heart, staring relentlessly at human shadows that, linked by a gentle magic of the hands, sometimes disappear for a good few minutes in the dance hall or in the bathrooms...

The Lord of the Groin raises his voice, battling the music that wears out the eardrums; he manages to win the attention of his friends and a few people nearby. He has the breadth of a storyteller and doesn't fail to brag about it. With a track record flowered in success over his twenty-year career, he shares that he had the habit, from a very young age in the countryside, of going to tell stories—which he sometimes invented himself—upon special invitation in *rara* parades, those groups of traditional Haitian music, in plantation squads, drudgeries, at wakes or any kind of festivity, occasions of popular taste. It always earned him something, at least a bottle of *clairin* was reserved for him. A champion of shots, he was pleased with such a salary.

As if to better pour words into the ears of his audience, he gulps down a large swig of beer and immediately enters into the story that is burning his tongue this evening.

It's the story of a female dog strolling the outskirts of the Champ-de-Mars in the middle of the night. Not just any dog, but one of those who've freed themselves to walk the interstices of the street, those whose body traverses the intricacies of the city, who've known everything under the sun and the stars. She passes a male dog running, stops him to chat. Why is your tail

between your legs like that, what's going on?
The male dog tells her that he's in danger. Cops
just wasted bullets into the air to send me away,
afraid I was barking while they raped a boy in
their car. So the female dog indicates to him
that she understands him. I want to believe you,
fellow, but it's not the first time I've seen you like
this, always with your tail between your legs.
No, replies the dog, that's not true at all, I swear
that there's at least one situation where I'm not
like that, and I can prove it to you right away.
Go ahead, open your body to me, invite me into
your flesh, and you'll see I'll no longer have my
tail between the legs, but between yours…

The audience, amazed, would like more of
such stories. But the star of the evening
seems to have other plans.

There's time that dries up cravings, there's
the clear throat of sleepwalkers at the edge
of delirium. The table is full of empty bottles,
words are filling up in the mouths. The night is
in full swing on human heads, brutal in the midst

of drunkenness. The Lord of the Groin goes into action, he starts to move his waist, works up an impressive shimmy, sprinkling salt into the rhythm of the atmosphere, rides the moment to the point that silence seizes what was. The lines come together, the laughters in a choir, the crowd in the bar gradually refocuses around the man who's dominating the dance floor.

The waitress feels powerless, she's there to serve people but now it's the people who are serving her a destabilizing spectacle. She goes to see the bartender, who reminds her that customers are allowed to take the reins of the kingdom; they feel at home, it's good for business, let them do it, when you like the seed you have to tolerate its skin. The bartender loves these improvised shows, as long as the outcome isn't disastrous. You had to have seen him last week: like a spring sky, his face opened when a hostess climbed onto a table to delight patrons with a striptease that ended in nudity. He was happy and even wanted to hire the customer...

The Lord of the Groin continues his feverish odyssey, his frenetic gallivanting,

undressing over the applause and the enchanting
laughter. The crowd appreciates his movements,
pulls out all the possible cards to excite him,
to incite him to go further, even further.
Women leave the hearts of their girlfriends
and boyfriends creaking, and come to offer the
fireship of their backside to feed the flame of the
one who's doing his party piece in the heart of
the bar. Men address their asses and their naked
torsos. At times leaning lightly against a table,
his cock raised like a rebellious torch towards the
sky, at others standing with one foot on a chair
like a pissing dog, his kite firming up in an azure
flavored with sensuality, the Lord of the Groin
accelerates more and more, his hand condemned
to rub his penis at an impressive speed.

Women and men are here, the women's asses
are still here moving, slabs of flesh exploding
their shorts, the men are here massaging their
breasts to the rhythm of winks, the crowd
is there, the chant of the crowd is still here,
gorging on pleasure. The man in the center feels
supported, he accelerates, no doubt all the bodies
he has known up until now have descended
into his hips, all the carnal fires he has passed
through are reborn within him. He continues
his stroke, swallows up thousands of kilometers
towards the summit of his trance. This fiery cock

is the promise of a big wave. Eyes closed, the Lord of the Groin caresses his shout, letting his body spring into the lands of ecstasy. He blesses the ground with a flurry of slimy puddles, in memory of Orange Blossom.

n our headquarters, not far from the room with air conditioning, just hanging out like that to try to tame the void, I run into Half-Blood. He's a deportee, as they say of those whom the United-I-do-not-know-for-what-good-cause-States agree—no doubt helped by the fact of being a "great power"—to expel from their territory because they've violated laws, whose human usefulness is, however, little proven. Arriving there at five years old, Half-Blood didn't take a long time to discover what could do him good, was immediately drawn to this plant that is forbidden to be grown on a good portion of the earth; soon he was rolling leaves of it endlessly, and it did him a world of good, that thick cloud that you release through your nostrils by pulling on the stick with the fiery-red ass. It was against his parents' wishes, who preferred that he instead conform his breath to a social environment that fears more than anything the smell of this thing that couldn't be more natural. He thus had been smoking marijuana since the evening of his childhood and at some point found it important to sell it, just to allow more people to get ahold of it. But the police, having understood nothing of his approach, ended up tracking him down. After two years in prison, which brought him into his thirties—he doesn't consider it a sentence, since he composed a hundred poems there that he's still trying to publish—he was forced to return to the so-called country of origin deemed his, where he had no bearings and whose language had escaped him a long time ago. Not having the right to return to the country that wants its own signature on a whole continent, he ended up carving out a place for himself here, by buying cannabis from the Angel of Metal to resell to the inhabitants of Cité Paille, a neighboring district just three kilometers from the City of God. I think that now he feels so good here that he no longer thinks of leaving. Whatever. On the off chance, I vaguely ask Half-Blood if he could help me get to New York without having to mess with all the paperwork that I've got a one-in-ten-thousand chance of obtaining—and still, this chance depends on the consul's mood. He boasts a big smile and begins to make of me a princess. I really admire you, my girl, you know, when I see you on that bench, there, in the back, chatting up the sky with a joint, I say: That's a fucking young lady right there! I contemplate

your insolent voice unfolding with the smoke
and I plunge back into this distant light of my
memory in the Bronx, this childhood where I
discovered the freedom that the country of the
Statue of Liberty believed it took away from me
by throwing me here. Honestly, you're awesome,
kid! What wouldn't Half-Blood do for you? The
guy who does it best in the city is a good friend
of mine. In fact, in this bag, I've got some greens
for him, he's always stocking up for the road.
He's leaving tonight, I just told you, right? If you
need a lot of days to get ready, then tonight is
dead. We need to leave if you don't want to miss
this opportunity, come on, he's in the area, the
captain, I'll introduce you!

I just smile, because Half-Blood doesn't even
give me the time to thank him.

ou'll be...
        I'm here, standing on the fault
        lines. Once again pulverized by a
gruesome song. Another episode of screams, a
new awful scene. The people seem to have found
a reason to revolt this time, they refuse to let
go of their leader, the most calibrated gangster
and therefore the neighborhood's shield. Just
the thought of him living in the area made the
neighboring little thugs, the *little rats* as we called
them, afraid of operating in the vicinity. The
Angel of Metal has just been killed by one of his
soldiers. We catch the killer. We are now on the
main road, at the edge of the huge waste basin.
There are more and more heads coming on the
set, to act, assist, or encourage others to act. The
show promises to be thrilling.

    I recognize him, our eyes meet, his gaze is
cold, his face is terribly lacking in pride. Behind
this human shell, one feels a struggling energy,
a bored spirit in Papa's skin, who never had the
chance to exist, never will, his powerlessness to
change the situation tortures him all the more.

Papa watches death invest his body by the force of his own kind. *You'll be alone at night.* I could very well sell this sentence back to him. That's justice over here. The people have long since ceased to believe in the one from the State, which is only a commodity. And then, anyway, it's not the business of the State, people know how to settle things themselves, with their arms or a simple magic trick.

*H*ere we are, rowing debris towards the red carpets. The violent red of gunshots. The red of neighborhoods condemned to savor their destitution. Eternal odyssey of blood. Dizziness rises to the surface. Here we are, another site of tears, another rain of fractures.

I look at the body, the urgency to die is palpable. He has little time left before becoming a dead body. I watch the crowd surrounding him, I hear the satisfying screams that cradle his road towards the infinite void. He tries to stay upright under the machete blows.

Only he knows why he did the unthinkable, why he killed the supreme leader just a few minutes ago—he didn't even have time to breathe in the smell of his crime, he was captured, disarmed, and now forced to suffer the worst. People, not wanting to mark themselves with blood, stop slapping and kicking and use objects: iron or wooden sticks, stones, shards of glass, electric cables. The symbol emerging from the context, the meaning of the act, what it means to give substance to the suffering of the other, what it means to hit someone with the stinging truncheon of death, the people don't really care about that, on the contrary, he's a criminal, they say, it doesn't matter to take his breath away, the dagger is legal.

And I, the child lost in the night, here I am, living this evil that I'm taught to legitimize, suffering the blows as much as Papa's body, seeing my stars fall into an unfathomable hollow. Here I am, body immersed in the shadows of the crowd, my proper name buried in this dirty common name of mortals. I want to shout, to shout the right to live ...

*E*ach blow is measured, to make Papa's suffering last. Spiteful perspective stretched without any embarrassment. A young man arrives with a bucket of motor oil and begins to spray the subject with it. The impact is revolting. A woman clears her mouth just for the pleasure of mixing her spit with the blood of the victim. A bread merchant stops and approaches; after finding out about the ceremony, he puts down his basket and advances towards the nucleus of the crowd, pulls out his penis and spreads a drizzle of piss over the body to be liquidated. Another young man returns from the stinking valley next door with a bag of shit, which he throws in the face of the Angel of Metal's executioner. The crowd applauds with a burst of laughter.

*M*ore machete blows. He falls to the ground, it seems like he's rushing to answer the call from above. More than one was waiting for this moment: the mutilated body is sprayed with kerosene. Fire. And it burns. It burns. Late Papa…

I feel my body burning too, my head sinking into a bottomless river. There remains of me this angel with butchered wings, this step stool of a pain more intense than that of the female body under the ax of the New Testament—*new* for the sole reason that it reformulates the horrors of the Old. The fact remains that my heart will soon be cut in half. A flood of hot tears rises from my orbits, causing me to touch my emotional share with my fingers. I leave, leaving behind me this flame dedicated to reducing Papa to nothing.

I barely make it fifty or so meters when a scream strays from the crowd and comes crashing down on the back of my head. I turn around and see the people dispersing, as if driven back by a terrible explosion. Following their disgusted gaze raised towards the sky, I see the root of the terror in the distance: Papa's inflamed body, in no greater hurry than this zephyr punctuating the approach of dusk, rises towards the clouds... They try to gather it with the help of a few bullets shot from his own work tool, but without success. The burning corpse eventually crumbles like smoke in the sky, leaving the minds of local residents blooming with questions that the legend of the mouth that gives and the ear that receives will surely find difficult to dissolve.

ou'll be...

My city, my neighborhood, my streets, my loved ones: broken veins in the race.

A bunch of broke footsteps. Breath-exhausting tremors.

Stumblings.

The fall of the solar impulses.

And the bodies locked in the arena of the condemned. And the bloated beings.

There's the throat-slitting, there's the strangulation. And the dotted lines at the rope's end...

Only pieces of silence seize my heart.

The wounds ooze from the burial cloth.

So many departures to consume.

Papa is no more, neither is the Angel of Metal: it's my hands that embrace nothingness, these hands that they've carved, these hands to sew my life through bullets, in the mortal periphery of blood. They didn't offer me any happiness, brought me nothing in life, but allowed me to live, and that is great.

Mom is no more: she's my sun that had fallen into a puddle of dirty water. Wide streams of dust secured to the eyelids, henceforth a washed-out sky torments my line of sight. Notebook of boos that revokes the candor of my ink.

Silence halfway around the world. I think about her, my moon, the star-girl who dances in my dreams. I think about her, without knowing if she does the same. She must spend her time fighting against the cold, grieving the warm arms of her father, whose absence will drag on forever. Maybe she spends her time in a living room, day after day feeding her love for sandwiches and television.

isfortunes tumble down my territory, catastrophes ravaging the fireflies of my horizon, creating a murky field. Memory wounded because my bearings are disappearing. My stars ruined, I'm off to pay homage to the void, to cherish their absence in the hollow of the days, like a voice drinking the cries in front of its tomb.

You'll be … You'll be alone in the great night. Am I at the end of the sentence? I should've never answered it. Why did Papa plant it in my head without teaching me how to grasp its branches?

My being, an abyss abandoned to the disturbing field of shadows. Not a wink from the sea to give flesh to my song of salt. For lack of lightning from my loved ones, I trace my path in strands of solitude. I give myself more reasons to love my gun, to go hunt lives for mine, which is no longer …

*W*hen hope falls, with its broken wings, and all lines run out of space, breath lets the pallor resonate. Like dust mocking the transparency of windows. This is the road narrated to my soles.

o doubt it was Papa who brought these strange objects over here before leaving, leaving never to return. I'm surprised that he could be interested in such things. But I know that no one else comes into our home. He's the one behind this. No cargoes this time, no guns. Not the tools of the red hand. Not the bloodletter's cards. I don't know what hurricane of tenderness hit him, he had another arsenal in mind. Perhaps he'd decided to keel over towards his reflection and grasp the other side of his being. Maybe he wanted to reattach his fragments and finally become someone else. He didn't get to do it, enveloped from this day forth by eternal nothingness.

I'm amazed by the objects. A turntable, records, and books. I attend to the record player, far more with my eyes than with my hands. I drop the needle randomly, and Coltrane starts on the track. I take the gun off my belt, grab a book, and sit on the cold floor. No thing of beauty on the cover, but it doesn't matter because I've never been interested in faces. I stop on the back cover, which takes me away for almost a minute.

The sound is delivered with softness, John Coltrane gives the wind the opportunity to tell me something, he whispers his copper disease, it heals me, transports me: *Blue Train*.

And then comes *good kid, m.A.A.d city*, a violent reflection of my state of mind in the voice and harsh language of Kendrick Lamar. The rhythm tears me apart, it shakes my head. I cannot miss the lyrics. The rapper lights up my conscience, it itches. I'm drained when my headlights are woken up. I don't know how to sing revolt.

The book remains in my hands, but I still haven't opened it. I turn off the record—the turntable must not appreciate this welcome for its first day in a house. Maybe what speaks to me doesn't heal me. Maybe only death heals.

I've got no desire to try another vinyl. I want to die. You have to die after Coltrane and Kendrick. I start to feel a little dizzy. I imagine myself succumbing to a violent fever. But clearly, nothing like that will happen to me here and now. I want to die. But pause. When *The Life Before Us* is in your hands, the thirst for words can be deadly. I wonder what's hidden between the lines of such a title. I don't know what the spirit hidden in the shadow of these ten letters has to say to me: Romain Gary. I open. Randomly, I fall on a part of a sentence that slices through me, that teaches me that "family means nothing and that some people even go on vacation leaving their dogs tied to trees and that each year there are three thousand dogs that die this way, deprived of the affection of their own." I don't feel like I'm any more than a dog.

You'll be . . . You'll be alone in the night.

I close the book, I don't have time to leaf through it, to continue reading. Night is approaching, I've got to finish packing my suitcase, because in a few minutes I've got to be at the rendezvous, near Route des Rails, not far from Cité Paille.

The waves are calling me, the sea, she's mine, I've got a rose to pick at the other end. I close my eyes to open them there. A dream awaits me beyond the waves.

ere we are on the verge of departure. We're a number that I don't waste my time counting, it'd take at least five boats, real ones, not hulls in distress like this old coffin boat that the hero of the probable future diasporas offers us. I should've figured it all out when Half-Blood introduced me to this man, this crazy man who, against all truth, we agree to call captain. I wonder if he's serious, to want to set sail in this uncontrollable human tide in a boat that didn't ask to be the pillar of a predisposition to catastrophe. We're past the meeting time but no one cares. Of course you shouldn't have counted on the punctuality of the residents of a country where one would always like the sun to rise a little bit later because we aren't done sleeping. People gather on the improvised dock, a thickening crowd that seems to ignore that it's as much a candidate for death as it is for the land that swears by the American dream. Students in need of university, degree holders from ruined lotto stands in search of work in a country where simply having a degree isn't a

criterion for finding any, minds stuffed with the
lies of a diaspora that hides its suffering so as not
to crush the idea of the country of fresh water,
folks who've sworn to get rich at all costs, others
who think that all foreign land is paradise—the
United States at the top of the list—those with
knees crushed by five hours of daily weeping
and to whom the ghost Jesus couldn't grant the
visa, men who came without wearing a condom
and who with their wives form a collective of
unemployed parents, in short, a desperate people
who claim to be fleeing poverty, in search of
a well-being that they're convinced they can
unearth in the starry country—I hope they have
the correct land of welcome. They all arrive, not
without nonchalance, loaded like tired donkeys
setting off from the vicinity of the Massacre
River towards some country lost behind the
mountains. Bags full of useless items, bowls
probably containing rice and chicken thighs
that will soon be devoured with pleasure, huge
suitcases that make you believe that some could
even take their homes with them, I mean, their
castles of chunked concrete blocks, their rabble
of failing sheet metal that keep our illustrious
slums alive.

Four hours after the initially planned
departure time, at the cost of long acrobatics, we

manage to pile into the gum tree. The evening
stretches out on the sea like a fake mural in front
of the heavens, a small wind comes to delight
the sail and now the boat, this shipwreck in
infancy, slowly breaks away from the coast, and
we finally leave. We think we're leaving, as if the
destination were within reach of our animated
bodies, some call it leaving, with ease. But we
all know, by habitual fate of these dubious
clandestine crossings, that no arrival will be
seen on the horizon. We aren't on a journey,
we're bodies perched on a destiny of dust from
which only a great miracle will tear us away.
Miracles, we believe in them here, to the point
of naming a street after them.

It can come with too little or too much wind,
and thus the prolonged duration of the trip or its
premature end, but there are all sorts of reasons
for ending up in the eternal void. Who doesn't
know the story of the lone captain? The legend
of the mouth that gives and the ear that receives
says that he set out for the Bahamas with about
forty weary souls from the native land, and that
he arrived there alone after having entrusted
them at times to the sea to lighten the boat about
to sink, at others to his belly to survive the two
unforeseen months of the journey. This story
remains a gaping wound that doesn't escape

the mind of anyone considering giving it a shot. Some still risk it in spite of everything, others, many, give up, forever, this terrible journey, which consists in crossing wild currents in close company of death. I remember hearing the Angel of Metal say one day, arguing his refusal to conquer the world by the way of the waters, that the sea is like a corpse on which one dances only at the risk of a terrible fall, because this blue-complexioned villain can abruptly wake up under your feet and force you to switch places with it. And that is enough to produce in me all the possible turmoils.

As I watch the old vessel zigzag under my tight heart and all these passengers who didn't decline the idea of clinging to it, an untouchable anguish shakes me. I think about my moon, who's waiting for me on the other side, and I regain strength. We make progress, a wave calls into question the life expectancy of the boat, and I fall back. In these moments when we're sailing towards the most distressing uncertainty, the wait is like a grain of silence sown on the waves, which we'll harvest at the other end of the shore in an inevitably piercing cry, one of light or dust, life or defeat, dawn or blood, blue sky or cloud too thick, of fulfilled hope or crowned nothingness.

The hours pass like a heavy spiral, where all sun slips away. High tides, dark surroundings, pale weather that makes me weak. Two, three days, tied up in eternity, such bearers of boredom. Two, three days, between the rage of the waves and the ferocious need to live with a crowd that doesn't have peace in common. Long country that I cross without lowering the mast of the eyelids. What kills me? Not my supply of water, bread, and ganja, which are about to run out, not the fact of having to do my business in plain sight and then throw it at the creatures of the sea, not this dead baby that was no doubt plucked by these depths full of inhumane vibes, but this whole continent of expectation and anguish, this immense curtain of uncertainty and terror that separates me from my moon. The nights drag on inside me, make me suffocate, as if my mouth was brushing endlessly against the screeching flute of death.

Two, three, four days, I finally see the silhouette of a slumber showing up that the dirty floor of the boat led me to believe couldn't be found. No sooner were my eyes closed when the fearsome lone captain arrived, his face resembling that of the teacher, Silence's father. He has already taken everything in a few days of travel. I'm the final passenger, he comes towards me as if I were his last resort to reach the shore. I see myself struggling under his weight and his knife. He manages to hold me down and devastates my crotch. When he raises his hand to plunge the blade right into my neck, I wake up, wounded in my being and in my deepest flesh. I shout to shake up the sailboat, to lift the depths of the seas. The passengers give me a weird look. I scream again. No, not me! I wasn't born under a star intended to feed jellyfish! Who'll die? Not me! Blessed name of the dead flesh, save me! Eat this monstrous dream!

In this cramped, rickety, filthy palace, which most passengers don't have the decency to fear, all sorts of challenges have targeted me. I was treated to the scents worthy of the remains of a dog around the corner of Champ-de-Mars but that, in reality, emanate from these human bodies that have surely not known water for weeks. I was treated to the incessant and never-silent anger of the captain, to the repulsive noise of mouths deprived of patience in the face of stale bread for several days. I endured the dubious stories of gossipers and friends, their prowess in wanting to tell the spiciest story, thus indulging in a din of fiery words in the name of neighbors to whom one lends fictitious declarations...I suffered the onslaught of all these delirious tongues, amplified by the disordered choir of whining children. I made my body take up all the positions that promiscuity allows, I wore out my gaze on all possible sides, participated in all the cries of the crowd, in all the complaints each time the boat brushed against a disaster. After five days of coping with boredom, fear, and all the imaginable emptinesses, my resources are running out. I feel myself dying, every second, ever since I have been aboard this freewheeling, headed-for-the-afterlife excuse for a boat. While rummaging through my belongings for the umpteenth time to check what I haven't yet tired of looking at, I remember that I had packed *The Life Before Us* in my bag. First smile of the trip, and you should see this moment when my face organizes itself other than by turning pale, it's like breaking the legs of the greatest despair. Leafing through the book, I come across an envelope. A quick glance, I see my name and my school's address, probably the mail was delivered there before Papa collected it. Anyway, it's impossible to send anything to me by mail, unless you have several pages to explain the address, which isn't one, unless you want to send the mailman to the biggest clusterfuck there is. I'm so excited to find out what's behind that envelope that I don't even wonder how I missed it when I opened the book at home—I should've leafed through it. A letter from Silence. My blood begins to boil. I feel all the faults of the earth rising in my body. I'm shaking. Correspondence from my moon. Something passes through me and raises a fiery flash in me, as if my heart were flying towards a sky on fire. Immense is the sea where I throw my being.

My Love,

I haven't stopped cumming. Since our magic of
human warmth, I haven't stopped cumming.
Since our bodies touched, I carry you alive
inside me, and each of my nights reminds me of
us, engaged in this first unforgettable orgasm.
A constant fire roams inside me, and each
morning, like dawn rising behind the mountains,
a shivering current unfolds between my legs: I
cum…I cum because this ultimate act that our
bodies fashioned in the bathroom of the church
lives inside me full-time. In these moments, I'd
tear in a second all the kilometers that separate
us, to plunge back into you.

I'm dying.

I'm dying over here, and to this, I know it,
only one reason: you don't exist in New York. I
looked for you in its wandering rumors, its lively
childhoods and its agitated gleams. I looked for
you under the tawny sheets of this city whose
real job is to crush people's thirst for peace. My
quest is in vain, the days betray me and the sun
that calls itself mine remains cold like the shores
of your absence.

I'm dying.

I'm dying, but I haven't told my mother
anything, I know she wouldn't understand me;
with all the churches in the world in her head

*and all these scriptures proclaimed holy by fools
on her lips, she can't listen to me. Given the red
mess that my face has become day by day, she
began to multiply her prayer sessions where my
name made the headlines, her litanies populated
by inconsistency to a god said to be powerful but
incapable of showing his ass in the hell that is
this world, despite an announcement launched
two millennia ago. Seeing that it didn't work,
my mother took me to a psychologist. The latter
speaks of the unbridled crisis of adolescence,
of an uncontrollably fluctuating personality,
of impenetrable withdrawal, and above all she
thinks that I still have to mourn my father in
Port-au-Prince before I can bury myself in New
York's lights. In addition, the lawyer who was
in charge of selling our old family home has
just told my mother that a hidden camera has
been discovered at the entrance, and that it could
contain footage of my father's assassination.
He says that only my mother can authorize its
viewing, and he ended up convincing her to return
to Port-au-Prince to urge the judiciary to open
an investigation.*

*So I'm going to go home, not for this matter
of justice, because I don't care: the only thing
that could appease me is to have the possibility
of killing the assassin with the very weapon that*

gave my father all the fortune of his veins. But I know that justice isn't for that, they won't let me respond to this desire. Only one reason is pushing me to return to this country that doesn't deserve the love of a little girl turned orphan in such obscure circumstances: to find myself in your arms again. I'm returning to reconnect with your fire, to enjoy the sound of cumming in your presence again.

Sending you kisses, and I'll be there in ten days to do it again with my tongue,

Your girlfriend.

JEAN D'AMÉRIQUE, born in Haiti in 1994, is a poet, playwright, and novelist. He received the Prix de Poésie de la Vocation for his poetry collection *Nul chemin dans la peau que saignante étreinte* and the Prix Jean-Jacques Lerrant des Journées de Lyon des Auteurs de Théâtre for his play *Cathédrale des cochons*. His first novel, *Soleil à coudre*, was published in France in 2021.

THIERRY KEHOU is a writer and literary translator based in Brooklyn, New York. His translation of Francis Bebey's novella *Three Little Shoeshiners* received support from the Bread Loaf Translators' Conference and was long-listed for the 2020 John Dryden Translation Competition. He is a founding member and board member of Lampblack.